Elizabeth

Also by Tasha Alexander

❧

Fiction

And Only to Deceive

A Poisoned Season

Elizabeth

The Golden Age

Novelization written by
Tasha Alexander
Based on the motion picture
screenplay written by
William Nicholson and
Michael Hirst

HARPERENTERTAINMENT

NEW YORK • LONDON • TORONTO • SYDNEY

HARPER**ENTERTAINMENT**

This book is a work of fiction. The characters, incidents, and dialogue are drawn from the author's imagination and are not to be construed as real. Any resemblance to actual events or persons, living or dead, is entirely coincidental.

HarperCollins books may be purchased for educational, business, or sales promotional use. For information please write: Special Markets Department, HarperCollins Publishers, 10 East 53rd Street, New York, NY 10022.

FIRST EDITION

Designed by Nancy Singer Olaguera, ISPN Publishing Services

Library of Congress Cataloging-in-Publication Data is available upon request

ISBN: 978-0-06-143123-4
ISBN-10: 0-06-143123-0

07 08 09 10 11 OV/RRD 10 9 8 7 6 5 4 3 2 1

1585—Spain is the most powerful empire in the world. Philip of Spain, a devout Catholic, has plunged Europe into holy war. Only England stands against him, ruled by a Protestant queen.

Prologue

He did not look like a king. More like an ascetic, swathed in black, but perhaps this was fitting for a man who had just accepted such a grave and holy mission, who'd sworn to put the Lord's will above human concerns. He abased himself before God, bowing low in the palace chapel—a lavish space, its opulence worthy of a cathedral, a perfect contrast to the utilitarian rooms of his private apartment. Art was for the glorification of God, not a pretty amusement. Full of the satisfying confidence that comes with divine direction, he rose, eager to begin.

The Spanish empire was the most powerful in Europe. Its *conquistadores*, men like Cortés and DeSoto, had no qualms about destroying the primitive natives they found in the New World, people foolish enough to trade gold for feathers, beads, any worthless trinket. They rejoiced as they melted into coins the false idols of these heretics. Yet as great as their desire was for wealth, it paled when compared to something of far greater significance. These warriors were also meant to be crusaders, and their king, Philip, put great value on the conversion of souls.

And it was souls that consumed his thoughts as he limped through lengthy corridors beneath gracefully curved ceilings—servants darting out of his way, pressing themselves against the walls—and into a salon, where courtiers bowed, silent at the sight of their ruler, instantly aware that something of great significance had come to pass. Philip did not acknowledge them, only increased his awkward pace.

The core of the Escorial Palace near Madrid may have been monastic, but its state rooms were suitably royal, full of ornate decoration: spectacular tapestries depicting religious scenes, paintings by Titian, Bosch, and El Greco. The furniture was elaborately carved from rare woods, and gilded plaster and frescos covered the vaulted ceiling, at the base of which religious statues sat, looking as if they were contemplating the holy work conducted below them on the floor.

Ministers and members of the court fell to their knees as Philip entered his most magnificent salon, his eyes searching for one person, uttering not a word until he'd found the priest. The Jesuits were a powerful order, known for their superior schools and missionary work, and their political influence was growing, not only in Spain but in Germany and France as well, their well-educated members natural leaders of the counter-reformation. The English, a heretic nation led by an excommunicated queen, feared them, for although the Superiors of the Order had hesitated to go into Britain, once they'd begun their mission, they would stop at nothing to protect Catholic souls.

"God has made His will known to me," Philip said, his voice full, authoritative. "The time for our great enterprise has come."

Robert Reston, clad in his holy robes, met the king's stare. "At last," he murmured, gratified and determined, but too disciplined to show any emotion. He was more radical than others in his order, a person unlikely to obey the mandate of his superiors, who insisted that Jesuits in England avoid all discussion of politics and never speak against the queen. Reston remembered all too well the brutal execution of one of his holy brothers, Edmund Campion, who'd met his death in England. There were moments when he envied his friend's martyrdom and other moments in which he longed to avenge his death. Hours of prayer did not take away the desire for revenge, confirming Reston's belief that it must not be wrong, not in these circumstances—instead, this marriage of personal satisfaction and holy work was a divine gift. All he had been waiting for was his king's order to begin.

From outside, the sound of cathedral bells rang, their rich tones competing with the cheers from the crowd in the plaza to fill the halls of the palace. Philip moved, instinctively regal, through open doors to a balcony, the cries of his subjects rising as he stood above them.

He did not wave.

He did not speak.

Only breathed and drank deeply the adoration flung before him.

Chapter 1

England had never before had a queen like her. Elizabeth was striking in appearance—fine red hair fell down her back and her pale complexion glowed—but it was her sharp intellect and quick wit that made her a queen worthy of her country. Her subjects were well-versed in the story of her tumultuous journey to the throne and admired her tenacity and her straightforward manner, never for a moment suspecting she was presenting them with a carefully crafted image of enduring strength.

"It's not safe." Lord Howard, second Baron of Effingham and cousin of the queen, spoke in a low, insistent tone as the royal barge glided along the Thames toward Whitehall Palace, a sprawling thousand-room castle that served as Elizabeth's official home in London. Concern chiseled deep in the creases of Howard's face, skin weathered by a youth spent at sea. "I tell you plainly, you will be murdered."

"You would have me stay always in the palace, protected

by an ocean of guards," Elizabeth said. She hated the very idea of it. It would be like a paralyzing death. "Never come among my people. I will not do that. They must see me."

"Every Catholic in England is a potential assassin," he said.

"And I will not be held hostage by imagined threats of violence."

"If your stance on the Catholic threat were harder—"

"I have said it before: I refuse to make windows into men's souls," she replied, watching the boat's bright silk canopy flutter as her rowers pulled, their oars rising and falling in perfect time. "There is only one Jesus Christ, and the rest is a dispute over trifles."

THE BANKS OF THE river were teeming with people, most of them smiling, waving, delighted to find themselves in such close proximity to their queen. Even the lower classes, living in poverty, adored her. To the wealthy and the new merchant class her policies brought more tangible benefits, not only monetary but intellectual, as education spread and new schools were built. And as English explorers set off for the New World, the boundaries of the beginnings of what might become an empire grew along with a heightened sense of excitement and possibility. London itself was a city brimming with opportunity.

Among the throngs of devoted subjects cheering the royal party no one took notice of two men—Anthony Babington and John Savage—who looked more intently than the rest, who stared with no admiration but hid their malice carefully as they faded into the crowd with little effort.

"Do you ever feel nervous?" Savage asked, watching the crowd. "About what we'll face if anyone discovers us?"

"It's quite a policy, isn't it?" Babington kicked at the dirt beneath his shoes. "Stay quiet and let the Protestant fools mislead the people and we won't kill you." The Catholic minority had been warned against irritating the queen lest she turn the sword of justice on them. Those who stayed out of politics and drew no attention to themselves were safe. The rest faced torture and the scaffold. "We're doing God's work. It is the queen who puts herself in a dangerous position by adopting heretical views."

"Yes. She must die." Savage hoped his companion did not detect the fear in his voice.

"And if it is God's will that she die, why should I be scared of the consequences for myself?" Babington asked. "If we are caught, the heretics will make us glorious martyrs. That is something I could never fear."

Savage swallowed hard. He agreed, in theory, with everything Babington said, but was finding the reality of it slightly harder to accept. He'd heard too many stories of joints dislocated by the rack, men crushed by the scavenger's daughter. And he'd seen firsthand what hours of hanging by the wrists did to his father. There was no mercy to be found in the Tower of London. These thoughts scared him, so he prayed, and God restored his focus, and they continued along the river, planning the details of the attack they hoped would change their world.

The boat had reached Whitehall, north of Westminster Palace. Elizabeth's father, Henry VIII, had extensively renovated the medieval palace, adding tiltyards for tournaments and tennis courts, creating for himself a perfect royal playground. The waters of the Thames lapped against the Privy Stairs as the queen's party disembarked to walk through mazes of courtyards and buildings whose very structure was designed to reflect the hierarchy of the court. Public rooms came first, but the farther one delved into the palace, the fewer people were admitted through the guarded doors. At the end were the queen's private apartments, where only a select few were ever allowed.

Elizabeth stalked into the Privy Chamber, within whose stone walls the business of the realm was conducted, where her most trusted advisors, her Privy Council, surrounded her. Sir Francis Walsingham had been ambassador to France before his appointment as principal secretary over foreign and domestic concerns, but he was also her spymaster, coordinating all covert operations. She'd given him the nickname Moor because of the dark tone of his olive skin, and he'd become a friend.

"Is this what I'm to expect today?" Elizabeth asked him as

she entered the room. "Endless talk of religious discord?" She knew it was unavoidable, that the fervent beliefs of her subjects, both Protestant and Catholic, could tear England apart. It was the same bloody battle raging across Europe, a battle set in motion when Martin Luther posted his *95 Theses* on the door of Castle Church in Wittenberg, Germany, and hardly slowed even by the implacable violence of the Spanish Inquisition.

"It is necessary, Majesty," Walsingham said. "But there is another matter—"

She saw the papers in his hands and cut him off. "Not now, Moor. We'll discuss it later. Much later." He had brought her another petition begging her to choose a husband—she'd recognized it at once. Marriage and religion, the two favorite topics of her ministers, the least favorite of hers. She liked to say that her father, who'd taken six wives, had married enough for both of them, but she alone appreciated the humor of this statement. "Let me deal with Howard and his concerns."

Walsingham bowed and stood to the side, watching as the queen joined her other advisors seated around a long refractory table beneath an enormous portrait of Henry VIII, the painted image staring at them through small eyes.

"The Catholic faction grows bolder every day, Majesty," Lord Howard said.

"Bolder how?" Elizabeth asked. This was Howard's typical stance, and she anticipated he would next bring up lingering memories of a Catholic uprising among the earls in northern England—a rebellion Howard had helped to quell—as a beacon of warning.

"The Spanish speak openly of Mary Stuart as Queen of England in waiting," Howard continued.

William Cecil, Lord Burghley, who'd been at her side from the time of her coronation, nodded. "She is dangerous, Majesty."

This was not the direction she'd expected the conversation to move, and she did not like it. The beginnings of anger crept into her stomach and she slapped her hand on the table. "Mary Stuart is a queen cast out by her own ungrateful nation." A revolt in Scotland years ago had delivered Mary from her third husband, James Hepburn, Earl of Bothwell, a brutal and abusive man, but left her a prisoner, forced to abdicate her throne to her young son, James. Escape to England had provided little respite.

"Mary Stuart is the arch-plotter at the heart of every Papist plot," Sir Christopher Hatton—whom she called Lids—said.

Elizabeth closed her eyes, stopped listening. She could recite his litany herself. The previous year, the former Scottish queen had accused him of being Elizabeth's lover, but she knew his opinion of Mary was not formed simply out of bias or desired revenge. Mary provided Catholics in England with a potential Papist queen, one ready to act, primed for sedition. Elizabeth should tread very carefully and take heed of the warnings her ministers brought.

She was so tired of all of it.

"Mary is my cousin. She is our guest. You will pay her the respect due to her rank." *Guest.* It was, perhaps, an extraordinary choice of word to describe a woman who for nearly twenty years had been shuffled from prison to prison. Her cells may have been in castles and country estates, yet they nonetheless held her against her will. But as exhausted as Elizabeth was by all this, she was no fool. She recognized the dangers posed by Mary. It was unfortunate, though, that her advisors refused to see the inherent difficulties caused by holding a sovereign queen prisoner.

"All Catholics are traitors," Hatton said. "Why do we leave them free to practice their Papist religion? They should all hang." *Free.* Elizabeth smiled at realizing that she was not the only one using ill-chosen words.

The public celebration of the Catholic mass was illegal, and though she tacitly tolerated its practice in private, this was a long leap from religious freedom, and she knew it. Furthermore, she'd let herself be persuaded to change the recusancy laws. Now, instead of being fined a shilling per week, those who did not attend Anglican services on Sundays were fined twenty pounds per month. It did not please her to do such things, but they were necessary. Still, she would not be pressured when she did not want to be.

"How many Catholics are there in England, sir?" she asked. Her face, the beginnings of wrinkles showing her age, was serious, her blue eyes rimmed by lashes so pale they were nearly white.

"Immense numbers, Majesty. Some say half the nation clings to the old superstitions." Hatton met her stare with an even calm.

"What would you have me do? Hang half the people of England, or just imprison them?" she asked. Walsingham still hung back, not entering the conversation, and Burghley had risen from the table to stand next to him.

Half the nation. A nation that remembered all too well the brutal religious persecution ordered by Elizabeth's predecessor and Papist half-sister, Mary I: burnings, torture, all hideous justice in the name of God. The Catholics had their turn at bloody power during Mary's reign, and the proud woman seated in the Privy Chamber had no intention of letting the Protestants follow, unchecked, the same ugly course. But spectacular executions were still far from uncommon, like those, four years earlier, when three Catholic priests—Edmund Campion, Alexander Bryant, and Ralph Sherwin—had suffered unspeakable torture in the dungeons of the Tower of London before they were hanged, drawn, and quartered.

They'd met a traitor's death, witnessed by faithful supporters who collected drops of the martyrs' blood and any other grisly relics they could. Supporters who would not soon forget how the law acted against holy men wearing the wrong robes. Religious persecution was far from finished.

"I would not have you hang all of them, Majesty," Howard said. "But we must show our resolution. We must act against the more extreme elements."

Skepticism leached through the heavy, white lead paint on the queen's face. "And how are we to know these extreme elements?"

"By their actions. By their plots and treacheries." There was an urgency in Howard's voice, an urgency that irritated the queen.

"Do we not have laws already against plots and treacheries?" She spoke forcefully, wanting no one to doubt her authority. "If they break the law, let them be punished. Until that day, let them alone."

"Until the day they rise in rebellion. Majesty, we have proven reason to fear every Catholic in the land—"

Elizabeth did not let Hatton finish. "Fear begets fear, sir. I will not punish my people for their beliefs. Only for their deeds. I am assured that the people of England love their queen. My constant endeavor is to earn that love."

She rose from the table, a swish of blazing brocade, exquisite lace and jewels, the air around her heavy with rosewater and musk. The gentlemen leapt to their feet, bowed. The conversation was over, the queen unmoved.

❧

AGAIN, THE ROYAL BARGE slid through the waters of the Thames. Again, Londoners on the riverbanks cheered at the sight of their queen, and she watched, giving at periodic intervals the slightest nod of her head, a slim acknowledgment of the pleasure she took at the devotion of her subjects. Traveling by river, particularly in a boat full of luxurious seats and fine silk cushions, was far preferable to subjecting oneself to the dirty misery of London's roads, whose dreadful condition made riding in a coach uncomfortable, if not impossible.

Bess Throckmorton, possessor of a captivating beauty that surpassed the exuberant glow of youth, had quickly risen through the ranks of the Ladies of the Privy Chamber to become the queen's favorite. Her full lips and delicate nose, flawless skin and blue eyes would tempt the most dedicated celibate, but it was her sharp mind that drew the queen to her.

Walsingham, across from the ladies, leaned forward. "You can't put it off forever. The people have presented a petition with over a thousand signatures."

Elizabeth could think of nothing she'd better prefer to put off forever than this petition. She had even hoped that he'd left the dreaded document in the Privy Chamber. She tried—and failed—to remember how many times she'd been given similar papers demanding that she marry. Once, Parliament had done it, saying that by marrying and having children, she would give herself immortality. The Speaker of the Commons had assured her that this was the single—the only—prayer of all Englishmen. But all that had done was make her wonder at the lack of imagination necessary to be able to think of nothing better to beg from God.

She disdained demands that she take a husband, whether they came in the form of a petition or were couched as thoughtful advice from her ministers. There had been moments—some long, some brief—in which she'd nearly succumbed to the charms of her favorite gentlemen, but she'd reigned alone for too long. She had no desire to share her power, wanted no master in her house, and she turned her attention back to Bess, brushing aside a soft lock of hair that had fallen over the girl's smooth forehead. "Don't hide your face."

"The bishops of Ely and Wells are saying that the continued sterility of Your Majesty signifies God's displeasure with us all," Walsingham said.

She did not reply, watching her Moor in silence before looking back to her companion. "We shall have to look out for a husband for you soon, Bess."

"Not too soon, my lady." Porcelain cheeks stained red.

"Don't you want to be married?" the queen asked.

"I'll want the marriage if I want the man."

She could tell Walsingham was trying to stifle all signs of frustration. His eyes bulged, but he was not slipping into the sarcasm to which he was prone. "You'll do as you please, of course. But at least look as if you've read their petition," he said.

"What sort of man do you want, Bess?" Elizabeth asked, continuing to ignore him.

Bess smiled, musical laughter escaping from her rose-colored lips. "A fine gentleman-like appearance."

"What does that mean? Tall?"

"Tall." The girl paused, thought. "An open face. Friendly eyes."

"Personally," Walsingham began, "I would advise you to keep the possibility open. Maintain uncertainty."

A vibrant spark filled the queen's eyes. "And good legs. You'll want good legs." The two women moved closer together, pleasure brightening both their complexions.

"And he's not to eat with his mouth open, or tell the same joke over and over," Bess said.

Walsingham spoke with more force. "At least enter negotiations for a contract with a foreign prince. Just to show the world that England still has friends."

A smile spread the queen's painted lips. "And sweet breath, Bess. So that you can kiss him without choking."

Walsingham's voice rose again. "To show the world that you may yet have issue—" This got her attention. Elizabeth struck him, her sharp hand delivering a solid blow. She relished the stinging sensation on her skin.

"Child. Say 'child.' You are talking like a bishop now, Moor. 'Issue,' indeed!"

"Child, then. I was being delicate."

Her voice fell as she grew serious. "There's nothing delicate about having a child. It kills women every day." All lighthearted joking and lusty pleasure flew from the barge and a tense silence settled on the party. Uncaring, sunlight continued its dance on the rippling water. Elizabeth watched it, untroubled by tension. Anything was better than discussing marriage.

When at last they'd reached their destination—no one having enjoyed the awkward remainder of the trip—they climbed off the boat and headed toward St. Paul's Cathedral. Elizabeth turned to Walsingham with a calculated smile, ready to reconcile with him. "If I did marry, you'd do well to remember it would not necessarily solve the problem of succession. A child of mine might not make a good heir. It could grow out of kind and become perhaps ungracious."

Walsingham opened his mouth to reply, but Elizabeth silenced him with a shake of her head and continued toward the steps of the cathedral. The long Gothic building loomed above them, taller than the other buildings of the city despite the fact that its spire had been destroyed by a lightning strike. Scaffolding surrounded the church as renovations, funded in part by the queen, were underway. Inside, the nave's Norman triforium and vaulted ceiling soared, though much of the splendid medieval decoration had been removed. No signs of Papist superstition and idolatry were welcome in an Anglican church.

But the reformists had left the stained glass, and Elizabeth looked up at the rose window as she entered, sent Bess back to her place among the other ladies-in-waiting, and then spoke, her voice hard but quiet, to Walsingham.

"I have darker concerns than marriage. Shipbuilders are being recruited in Spanish ports at double wages. The seawall at Dover is cracking. There's no money to rebuild our defenses. I don't need advisors to tell me my business."

"They care for your safety, Majesty. The threats to your person are real."

"And they know very well that if I fall, they all come tumbling down after me." She had reached the steps at the foot of the altar, lowered herself to her knees, and began to pray. Without turning around, she held a hand out behind her. Bess stepped forward, taking it at once, and knelt to join her queen in prayer. The warmth of the girl's hand brought a smile to Elizabeth's face. Surely friendship was a more reliable cure for loneliness than marriage.

Far from London, a ship drew into view of Dover's white cliffs. Birds dipped and soared, black streaks against the bright chalk, their sharp cries carrying far over the open water, and the slim green strip of land atop the high ridge called out to sailors elated at the sight of England. The weariness that had set in during their long journey home evaporated in an instant. Already they could imagine their homes, their wives, food that hadn't been stored in brine or dried until it was barely edible. Comfort was long overdue these men, and now that it was so close, they worked with an energy they'd not had in months.

They pulled ropes, unfurled the dingy canvas sails of their square-rigged ship. Every inch of the *Tyger* was battered and worn, its wood bleached from long hours in the sun, paint beginning to peel. But the ship was solid and returned from the New World carrying treasure and stories of endless adventure.

They'd skirmished with Spanish vessels and plundered more than a few. But they'd spent most of their time scouting out locations for future English colonies, because their captain's primary mission was to find a place suitable for permanent settlement—a city that would start the English empire, bringing glory to his country but also to himself. He'd decided on the island of Roanoke, a place where crops grew at astonishing speeds in the fertile soil and the natives they'd encountered were gentle and faithful, greeting strangers with no aggression.

The indigenous people were everything exotic, with their walnut-colored skin and clothing of leather. But they were far from uncivilized. They were farmers who cultivated fields, fishermen with boats. Their houses were built from cedar, surrounded by stockades made from tall logs whose tops had been sharpened to deadly points. Thomas Harriot, the expedition's scholar and scientist, had set to learning their language, Algonquin, and succeeded in teaching English to two natives who had decided to leave their tribal homes near Roanoke and go to England.

Manteo was a chief of the Croatoans, and Wanchese a high-ranking member of the Winginas. They'd entertained the sailors admirably during the journey home, Harriot translating their stories when the natives' English failed them. But now, as their time at sea was drawing to a close, they were protesting loudly in their own language as well-intentioned but thoughtless sailors forced them into stiff coats of brown taffeta.

"Leave him alone, Mr. Calley." The ship's captain, Walter Raleigh, skin bronzed from the journey, curly hair tousled by the wind, crossed to his first mate, who was having no success getting a hat over Manteo's thick hair.

"Scare away all the ladies, sir. Paint his face white, I think," Calley said, his own face tanned nearly as dark as the natives'.

Though Raleigh was no less weather-beaten than his men, he could not be taken for anything short of their leader. It was in his walk, his posture, the steady and commanding calm in his green eyes. He'd fought with the Huguenots in France—had been a devoted Protestant since his youth—and had helped put down a rebellion in Ireland. But he was also a poet and a man of science. Manteo and Wanchese watched as he approached them with a quick, courteous bow. The natives smiled, and Raleigh threw an arm around Manteo's shoulder, steering him to the foredeck.

"England, my friend. The mother of us all, and our sweet home." Dover's cliffs were closer now, white rising from the sea, gleaming against the sky.

"And not before time," Calley said, the rest of the sailors on deck shouting hearty agreement.

"As soon as she's seaworthy again we'll be back to your

world, my friend." Raleigh smiled at Manteo, who grinned back but gave no reply. The *Tyger*'s crew did, however, answering their captain with a chorus of groans.

"Don't worry, boys," Calley said, then turned to Raleigh. "You'll need your warrant from the queen, sir. They say it's not so easy to see the queen. They have officers at court, they say, whose only job is to keep people like yourself waiting. Sometimes for years, sir. They say." Hopeful-sounding murmurs flew from the sailors.

Raleigh filled his lungs, pulling in the clean English air as deep as he could. He'd always considered patience the most overrated of the virtues, and it was said the queen was not immune to the charms of adventurers. If he could win her favor . . . his eyes turned away from Dover back to the open sea, his mind full of visions of a new colony. He didn't relish the idea of playing sycophant, but if it gave him the means to found a civilization, it would be well worth it. He could think of no other way to obtain what he'd need: money, more ships, more sailors, and people willing to live in the New World.

And yes, as Calley reminded him, he would have to have a warrant from the queen. That would be his first priority. Queen Elizabeth. What could he do to impress her? To get her attention, and quickly? A crooked smile crept onto his face. This might be an adventure all of its own. He called to his first mate.

"Well, Mr. Calley, we'll see about the queen. But for now, let England know we're back!"

Raleigh's sailors cheered, stomped their feet on the deck, and he felt the pulse of their enthusiasm in his chest. The gunmen stationed in front of the ship's eighteen cannons stood, watching for his signal. He raised his hand, dropped it, and the guns fired toward the distant white cliffs. The *Tyger* was home.

Chapter 2

It was impossible not to be drawn outside when the sky turned that perfect shade of blue that was at once cool and warm and looked as if it could swallow whole the crisp clouds that dared cross its broad spaces. Elizabeth had spent much of the afternoon watching her courtiers playing tennis on her father's courts. She picked her favorite competitors and gave them handkerchiefs to indicate her support, but she paid only half-attention to their games. After supper, she'd sat through a disappointingly tedious play—there had to be someone in England capable of producing something more entertaining—and then she and her courtiers had danced in the Presence Chamber.

La volta, with its jumps and turns, had always been her favorite dance. She loved the way her heart raced from both the exercise and the feeling of strong hands around her waist, the intimacy of a handsome face close to hers. But tonight, though she was as exuberant as usual, she noticed that her first partner—a young earl who'd only recently come to court—though attentive, was smiling at one of her ladies.

"You like her?" Elizabeth asked, as he spun her around.

"Margaret?" he asked, and she did not like how quickly he'd responded with a name. "She's a sweet girl, but nothing compared to you, Majesty. How could a man's attention be diverted, even for an instant, when he's with such an engaging beauty?"

They were pretty words. She expected nothing less. But they meant little when the man uttering them was, in fact, diverted by someone else. Her second partner, a duke from the North, threw her high as she jumped.

"You're an excellent dancer," she said.

"It must be a gentleman's priority to dance well if he aspires to such a regal partner," he replied, spinning her furiously. "I practice daily, my head full of thoughts of you." Ordinarily, his speech would have pleased her. But tonight she noticed it was too rote, too memorized, too impersonal. She could not fault the way he spoke, his tone, the expression on his face, yet there was something beginning to tug at her, something uncomfortable that was keeping her from feeling the full delight of la volta.

The next man to stand up with her was Sir Christopher Hatton, who, before his appointment to the Privy Council, had courted the queen. His letters were the most beautiful she'd ever received. She could still remember his words:

Would God I were with you but for one hour. My wits are overwrought of thoughts. I find myself amazed. Bear with me, my most dear sweet Lady, passion overcometh me. I can write no more. Love me, for I love you.

The memory of it brought a smile to the royal lips, and Elizabeth relaxed in his arms as they danced. "Sometimes, Lids, I think you're the finest dancer I've known," she said.

"I've not the vigor I used to," he said. "We're neither of us so young anymore, are we?"

"I show my age?" She bristled.

"Not at all, Majesty. You are like a living miracle. Your face is as lovely as when you first ascended to the throne. It is as if you're entirely immune to time's hands. How do you manage it?"

"I don't believe a word you say, Lids."

And for the first time, she wasn't saying such a thing to flirt. There was no question that her courtiers adored her, that the men vied for her attention the moment she entered a room; they all desired her, longed for her favor, wanted to be her favorite. But she was beginning to suspect that the affection they rained upon her lacked a certain sincerity. Not of attitude, but of depth. She'd always known that men were attracted to her position and what it enabled her to give them, but they were also captivated by her wit, her intelligence, her energy—there was no other woman at court who could compete with her royal charms. Only now, it was beginning to seem that *royal* was more important than *charm*.

She was suddenly tired, and with a flick of her wrist stopped the music and stormed to her bedchamber. Her ladies had removed her heavy gown, corset, petticoats, and farthingale, then slipped a soft shift over her head. She sat in front of a mirror flooded by candlelight, watching Bess remove her thick makeup.

"Lines round my mouth," the queen said, tracing them with a single finger as she spoke. "Where did they come from?"

"Laugh lines, my lady," Bess said.

"Laugh lines? When do I laugh?" She had laughed, of course. By herself, with her ladies, with her favorite gentlemen. But now she doubted the sincerity of all of them. Robert Dudley had loved her, of that she could be confident, and the truth was, she still adored him. Her Eyes, the love of her youth, the man she'd desperately wanted to possess. She'd made him the first Earl of Leicester—the highest peerage she'd created during her reign—but he'd disappointed her over and over. There had been rumors of a secret marriage to Lady Douglas Sheffield, but he'd denied them and she'd believed him. Eventually.

But he did marry, and he did it in secret, and he lied to her about it. His wife wasn't Lady Sheffield but Lettice Knollys, her cousin, and she'd expelled them both from court after she'd discovered their deception. In time, she forgave him. It seemed nothing could entirely sever her connection to him; it ran too deep.

It was a pity he'd married, though. She never liked her friends or councilors to divide their affections between her and their wives. Not because she was jealous, of course—what cause would she have for jealousy? No woman shined brighter than she. She did not like marriage because she'd found that wives made gentlemen tedious, and tedious she could not tolerate.

After Leicester, there had been her Frog—François, Duke of Alençon—whose proposal of marriage she'd accepted, then quickly rejected, the match opposed by many at court, Leicester among them. She remembered the look on Robert's face when she'd told the French ambassador to inform his king that Alençon would be her husband. She'd kissed the duke—in front of the court—and given him a ring, accepted one in return. But had she loved him, this man nearly twenty years her junior? She recited to herself the lines of poetry she'd penned after he left her court: *I grieve and dare not show my discontent, / I love and yet am forced to seem to hate*. Her heart may have hurt, but she had never regretted the decision to keep the crown hers alone.

It was the right thing to have done, the best for England. And, by definition, what was best for England was best for her. She sighed, wishing that best didn't have to correlate with lonely.

"I feel alone tonight, Bess," she said.

"I'm here with you, Majesty. And you had the entire court enchanted when you danced tonight."

"They've no choice but to be enchanted. I would allow nothing else."

"They'd be enchanted regardless," Bess said, leaning close. "You're exquisite."

Elizabeth stared into the mirror. "I was, once." She touched fine lines next to her eyes. "There ought to be a magic way to erase these."

"You don't need any such thing."

"You're so young, Bess. You can't yet imagine time etching itself on your perfect face. You still think yourself immune." She reached for the girl's cheek and started to laugh. "Be glad, my friend."

"Whatever I am, it's nothing compared to all you are," Bess said.

"True," Elizabeth said. "But that is perhaps why you will find more happy contentment than I ever have." She walked to her bed and slipped between the smooth sheets; Bess pulled closed the bed's painted silk panels, and the queen listened as the girl left the room, the door shutting with a soft click. She was left in silence, a comforting, perfect sound after the chaotic energy of the court. There were benefits to being alone, undisturbed.

She fell asleep quickly, but the easy warmth that came with the remembrance of old loves was short-lived. Nightmares stalked her, and she awoke in the middle of the night, panting, horrified by the images in her head—half-broken bodies, death, and an ocean red with blood. She opened her eyes but couldn't focus. The immensity of her ornate bed engulfed her, and the voice from her hideous dream seemed to echo through her chamber:

Elizabeth! The angels weep for you, Elizabeth!

It was Philip, her former brother-in-law, her sister's husband. She had always hated the sound of his voice. Beads of sweat covered her forehead, and her shift was tangled and twisted between her legs. She sat up, panting, and whipped the curtains of her bed open, half-expecting to see her Spanish nemesis waiting for her. There was no one, of course, but she hardly trusted her eyes.

Her bare feet sank into the thick carpet as she started to pace the room, pausing only to look out the window at a forlorn sliver of moon. Thoughts bombarded her, but she could make no sense of them and retreated into a state of detached consciousness, vague pictures of Spain polluting her mind. She'd never visited the country but tried to imagine the geography, the people and their houses. Most of all, though, she imagined the army, and a fleet of ships that could bring it to England.

Tugging at her hair, she considered the motivation behind these visions. There was no question that Spain was a threat to the prosperity of her realm—it had been this way for years. So, why nightmares now? Why now, when she'd begun to feel as if a hole was gaping in her heart and wasn't sure how to fill it? She opened the window and held her hand in the night air, the cold breeze like a salve on her too-hot skin.

She would speak to the Spanish ambassador tomorrow, consult with her Privy Council, make sure that she was doing everything possible to strengthen her position. Her mind began to clear and the shards of unsettling fear that had come with her nightmare dissipated. She felt the calm that came from being in control and tipped back her head.

She would not tolerate Spanish threats, even in dreams.

Far south of England, light fought for passage through a dense forest, ancient trees blocking its progress. The sun the trees could stop, but they had no defense against the rhythmic motion of axe and saw wielded by an army of foresters. The hum of blades and the crash of falling limbs sent birds and animals scattering, until the only living creatures to be found were the men wreaking this havoc. A dark carriage, royal insignia on its sides, surrounded by a mounted entourage of well-armed knights, flew down a narrow road cut into the woods.

"'Elizabeth, you are leading the souls of your people to hell. Turn back. Marry me and save England.' I spoke to her just as I speak to you now." Philip smiled at his daughter. The infanta, Isabella Clara Eugenia, only twelve years old, smiled back at the father who, despite a reputation for coldness, had always rained affection on her.

His first son, Don Carlos, was deformed, with a hunched back and scores of physical and mental problems. His mother, Maria of Portugal, died soon after the child was born, and was spared the heartbreak of the boy's madness. Philip never despised Carlos, tried to train him to be a king, but to little avail. Stories of the prince's cruelty to animals and women circulated through court, as did rumors that he would not be able to have children. In the end, raging mad, he'd plotted against his father and was put in prison, where he died, only twenty-three years old.

Philip's second wife, Mary, Queen of England, gave him no child, and he scowled thinking about her, how he'd been led to believe she was a great beauty. How his first sight of her had taught him that portraits lie. She might have saved him from this Enterprise entirely had she done her duty and provided an heir. After Mary's death, he married Elisabeth of Valois, sister of the king of France. She was the mother of Isabella and her younger sister, Catalina Michaela. A fourth wife—his niece, Anna—provided a son, also named Philip, who so far had proven himself nothing but lazy and uninterested.

Isabella was his bright star, a smart, engaging, beautiful girl. She had with her today a favorite doll, more like a dressmaker's model than a toy, fashioned to resemble England's queen. Philip met the child's smile, then looked away, out the window, a faint shudder rippling through him at the sight of the ravaged landscape, immense piles of timber. "Every tree that falls hurts me." He squeezed his hands together. "I lose a part of myself. I am cursed with sensitivity. I feel too much."

Across from the king, Father Robert Reston's expression beamed beatific pleasure as he watched the progress. "Your Majesty has a merciful soul."

"I sacrifice my country's forests to save the souls of a lost nation. That is true mercy. England is lost to darkness, Father. I bring light." The smell of smoke seeped into the carriage, coming from the fires raging as branches, now useless, burned in clearings that were rapidly replacing forest.

He would build ships with these trees, ships that would carry an army to England and rescue the subjects he'd left behind when his late wife, Mary, queen of that country, had died. Elizabeth, the princess, now queen, had always tended toward the heretical. It was a disappointment that he'd not been able to convince her to marry him after her sister's death. There would have been none of this nationalizing of Protestantism, no putting at risk the eternal fate of so many souls. He mouthed a quick prayer of thanks, feeling blessed that God had shown him how they could still be saved.

The carriage passed close to the fires, the orange light of the flames reflecting on Reston's face at the window. "The light of purifying fire," he said, half to himself, then fixed his stare on the king. "My time has come, Majesty. Send me home."

Philip nodded, silent. Reston would go home and a new queen—a Catholic queen—would sit on England's throne.

Mary Stuart and her ladies had arrived at their latest prison on Christmas Eve, six months ago. Another house more like a castle—this one protected by a moat—another cell. Mary had spent her first four weeks at Chartley Hall ill, confined to bed. But now, summer had arrived, and with it, hope. One of her ladies, Annette, waited in the garden, a tiny Skye terrier yapping at her feet, his barking growing more excited when the laundress arrived, looking anxious, her eyes pinched. She handed Annette a letter, folded small, then curtsied and left. Annette wasted no time. She returned to the house, the dog scampering ahead of her, both eager to find their mistress.

Inside, locked in a well-furnished room, the former queen of Scotland sat embroidering a pink satin petticoat, around her a retinue too small for a woman who had been queen: three ladies-in-waiting and a chaplain. Mary was still beautiful—auburn hair and mesmerizing blue eyes, dignified and regal. She lacked only a crown and a throne and authority. Not small points, but points she believed could be overcome. Especially now.

"This is so pretty I'm inclined to send it as a present to my dear cousin Elizabeth." It would not be the first gift she'd sent the English queen: elaborately embroidered petticoats and kirtles, wigs, any lovely thing Elizabeth might like. Elizabeth had sent presents in return but, despite Mary's repeated requests, would not agree to see her cousin, who had now been in England for eighteen years.

Annette entered the room and knelt before her mistress, holding out the letter. "My queen."

Mary took the paper, her hand steady as she deciphered the note. "Our friends write to give us hope." She was used to her supporters scheming for her release, expected that loyal Catholics would do what they could to put her on the throne. But this latest plan brought hope far greater than any other: these men had gained the support of Spain.

Stepping forward, Annette spoke in a low voice, heavy with a French accent. "Soon England's true believers will rise up against the bastard usurper Elizabeth and slit her throat and throw her down to hell."

"That's enough, Annette." Mary sounded serious, but her eyes danced and there was laughter on her lips. "Slit her throat? Please."

"And when the bastard usurper is dead, my lady will be queen." Annette's smile was more than a little gruesome in its exuberance, but Mary relished the show of loyalty, knowing that if Elizabeth were gone, she would have a stronger claim to the English throne than anyone. She opened her mouth to reply and was silenced by a sharp, warning cough from her chaplain. The warden of Chartley Hall entered the room. Knowing full well that he appreciated his captive's beauty, Mary gave him a teasing smile.

"Here's my scholarly jailer. How bored you must be, sir, by such dull company." She held out a soft hand for him to kiss, putting the other, holding the letter, behind her back for Annette to take and hide.

Sir Amyas Paulet opened the book he was carrying. "Beauty is never boring, ma'am. In the words of the poet"—he started to read—"*Her cheeks like apples which / the sun hath rudded / Her lips like cherries charming / men to bite / Her breast like to a bowl of / cream uncrudded*—"

"Enough!" She was careful to imbue her tone with a deliberate harshness, leaving only the smallest hint of flirtation in her voice. "You take liberties."

"The poet Spenser, ma'am. Not I."

She dropped her eyes, paused for a calculated instant, then looked up at him. "But you allow me no liberties."

"Command me. I am your servant."

"I suspect you of being determined to keep me for yourself." Seeing that he was about to speak, she put a finger to his lips, silencing him. "Speak to Elizabeth again. Tell her my heart aches to see her." She held up the petticoat she'd been embroidering. "Tell her how I pass my time in my lonely prison."

"Charming, ma'am." Now it was his turn to pause, but there was nothing deliberate about it. He was flustered. "Distractingly charming."

Enjoying his response, Mary ran her hand over the cool silk, caressing it, then pressed it against her body. "Such a pretty undergarment. But for whose eyes?" Sir Amyas only stuttered, incoherent as his prisoner watched him, wicked mischief behind her smile. She could afford to play now that men of action had begun their plan.

❧

On a small back street in London, the pistol weighed heavy in John Savage's hands as he examined it in detail, its smooth wooden curves and cool metal barrel elaborately decorated, artful beauty at odds with deadly purpose. "Show me how to load it," he said. He'd never held such a weapon before—he'd grown up in the country, the son of a gentleman, but a poor one. A poor one who had not the sense to hide his faith, who'd been arrested and released, but not after first having suffered a brutal interrogation. A man whose complacent forgiveness of those who'd harmed him had spurred his son to action.

The armorer took the gun in his rough hands, knuckles swollen with arthritis, skin discolored, and began the fiddly process of loading it. He measured powder from a horn, pouring it without spilling even one grain. "So what's it for, my young friend? Not for shooting rabbits, I'm guessing," he said, pushing the wadding and an iron ball the size of a hazelnut into the barrel.

"We live in dangerous times," Savage said, studying each of the armorer's actions, memorizing what he would need to do to arm the weapon on his own.

"We do that. They say the Papists are getting ready to murder us all, like the Pope tells them." No one in England was ignorant of the violence Protestants had suffered in Europe. Thousands were killed in France during the St. Bartholomew's Day massacre, and the Pope, Gregory XIII, had rejoiced. Gregory and his successor, Sixtus V, were both strong supporters of the king of Spain, whose brutality gossips painted as legendary.

Rumor said that as Philip sat, gleeful, watching heretics burned at the stake, he'd taken no small dose of pleasure in the bloody work of the Inquisition. And rumor said that he was ready to bring what he considered the true faith to England, and with it, his fires to burn those who would not accept conversion. Rumors. Rumors that Savage knew to be false. It was the Protestants who were dangerous, who spread these lies.

The armorer handed the pistol, now loaded, to Savage, who reached for it with trembling hands. "Afraid of the Papists, are you?"

"I fear no man," Savage said. "Let others fear."

"Right, right. That's the attitude."

"The truth eventually comes out. It can't be hidden forever. Their day may come sooner than they know."

"*Their* day? Who do you mean?" The armorer, muscles clenching as he looked at his customer, reached for the gun. "Give me the piece."

"I must have it." Savage's voice was steady, but his body betrayed him, refusing to remain calm, shaking as he clutched the pistol to his chest.

"I'll see you hang first," the armorer said. Trembling, Savage raised the weapon to its maker. His finger, slick with sweat, pulsed on the trigger. He pictured the stooped form of his father—evidence of the end result of violent hatred—and unexpectedly found that he could not bring himself to fire. He felt like he would choke, and ran out the door.

Outside, he crossed the street, still running, feeling guilt, but not pausing to meet the eyes of a familiar figure, a Jesuit priest. Reston gave no indication that he recognized the fleeing man, just started for the shop, where the proprietor, trembling, was sitting, eyes closed, drawing a long breath.

"Who are you?" the armorer asked, looking up at the sound of footsteps.

"I ask your forgiveness." Robert Reston stepped forward and without hesitation twisted the man's neck, not flinching at the hideous sound of snapping bones, the sight of the armorer's head hanging limp.

The souls of England's faithful would soon be released from the grip of their heretic queen.

His king would be pleased.

His God would be pleased.

Chapter 3

Elizabeth walked every Sunday, processing from the Presence Chamber to the Chapel Royal, crowds gathering to watch, standing in deep rows, the mood jubilant. She always appreciated the adoration of her subjects. Sometimes they were at Whitehall, sometimes St. James' Palace; the location did not matter. The Chapel Royal was not merely a building but also the priests and choir who attended to her spiritual needs, and they served her wherever she might be.

A young courtier pushed forward, stepping close to her.

"Majesty, you are breathtaking today," he said, bowing with a flourish. As always, she'd selected her clothing carefully, choosing gowns and jewelry that would shine through the crowd and draw all eyes to her. She'd been particularly satisfied with today's combination, a stunning cream-colored gown with the heavy gold and jeweled chains hanging from her neck.

"We thank you," she said, hardly looking at him until she realized it was the Earl of Essex, Robert Dudley's stepson, who could not have been a day over eighteen.

"Every man in England weeps not to be at your side," he said.

She gave him a smile, liking the enthusiasm in his voice. It sounded sincere and boosted her mood considerably. When she spotted a little girl holding a bouquet of flowers in her hands, held back by a crush of people, she stopped and pulled the child forward, bending down to hear her speak. Around her, the crowd cheered, making it impossible to decipher the girl's words. Elizabeth stood at her full height and motioned for silence.

Her subjects responded at once, falling quiet. Perfect gratification.

Two of Walsingham's agents, covert, watched the spectators as they moved for a better view. They were careful, but so was someone else. A man keen to draw no attention to the bag he carried, a bag heavy for its size.

God bless Your Majesty!

God love you!

See her sweet face!

Her people fell to their knees, reached out to touch her as she neared them. Babington hung back, unobtrusive, taking note of the wall of well-armed bodyguards surrounding their royal charge. He knew exactly what to expect—he and

Savage had monitored the scene for weeks, planned their course of action. But Reston, without explanation, had sent him alone today, forced him to leave Savage behind.

He watched the guards pass, followed by courtiers and ladies-in-waiting—the queen's protectors masking her almost entirely. His breath quickened as he started to reach inside the bag, feeling for the gun. He moved forward, easing his way to the front of the crowd, halting suddenly as a scuffle started. He strained to see through the throngs of people, half-expecting to find someone on a mission as grim as his. Would Savage have disobeyed Reston and come on his own?

It was not Savage.

Instead, he saw a gentleman, dressed with not quite the same level of finery as the others near the queen. His fingers were covered with rings, but he wore no hat, and his curly hair was disheveled by the breeze. His doublet, though not cut from common cloth, looked dingy compared to those around him, and his appearance altogether lacked the polish of a courtier. But as Elizabeth approached him, he'd jumped forward and, with a swish, snapped the cloak from his shoulders and lowered it to the ground in front of her.

"A PUDDLE IN THE way, Majesty," Walter Raleigh said, a smile full of charm lighting his face as he smoothed his cloak on the ground. He seemed to take no notice of the guards coming toward him. And there was no need to. At the slightest sign from the queen, they'd stopped.

Elizabeth's eyes swept the man in front of her, and she nodded appreciatively at his handsome face and fine legs, smiling as she checked the ground. There was no sign of any puddle. "A puddle?" She met his gaze, her stare cool, and stepped on the cloak, shaking her head.

The guards fell back into their positions, and as the royal party continued on its way, one lady of the Privy Chamber looked back at the sea captain, throwing him a smile that, along with her shining eyes, sliced through him. Raleigh shrugged at her, picked up his cloak, and stood gazing after the queen until the doors of the chapel closed behind her.

He turned, found Calley—who'd hung back from the excitement—and put his arm around him. "She spoke to me. You have to give me that."

"Oh, I do," the first mate answered. "The queen spoke to you. One word—but she spoke," the first mate replied.

"Two words."

"You're made. A dukedom at the very least."

"Did you see the girl behind her?" His breath caught in his throat as he thought of her smiling at him. "I've been at sea too long."

Inside the chapel, dancing candlelight filled the dark space, illuminating its high stone arches as Elizabeth made her way to the large altar. The most powerful woman in the world knelt, supposedly at prayer, but her mind was elsewhere. She bit her lip and smiled, murmuring with amusement. "A puddle . . ."

ACCESS TO MANY OF the rooms at Whitehall depended on either a person's rank or favoritism of the queen, but every courtier could come into the Presence Chamber, a room splendid in magnificent grandeur and crowded every day with competing factions, each waiting—most in vain—for the queen's attention. Carved and gilded mahogany paneling covered the walls, the marble floor gleamed brighter than silver. Forming a canopy above and hanging down behind the brown velvet throne inlaid with diamonds was an elaborate tapestry showing Elizabeth's coat of arms, with three lions passant guardant, fleurs-de-lis, and her motto, *Semper Eadem*—Always the Same.

Those gathered to see her were no less spectacular than the room: the courtiers were dressed in bright velvets, jewels covering gowns and doublets, rings on every finger, feathers in the ladies' hair. With them, the Spanish ambassador, Don Guerau de Spes, stood in the middle of a group of his countrymen, his foot tapping impatiently as Elizabeth listened to her advisors, while an architect stood in front of her, drawings in his hand.

"I'm getting reports of riots in Paris. Mobs killing Protestants," Walsingham said, coming to her side, quietly briefing her. She had turned, ready to listen to him, when Lord Howard stepped closer, trying to persuade her to look at three small portraits, sent by would-be suitors to the queen, standing on easels.

"A French prince, Majesty," he said. "Cousin to the king."

"I'm told his breath smells." She went back to the architect. Unrest in France could lead to danger in England. "You have the plans for the new docks?"

"Here, Majesty." She studied the papers he handed to her as Walsingham continued to press her, his voice low.

"A Franco-Spanish alliance against us would be a disaster." Henri III, king of France, a Catholic, had courted Elizabeth to disastrous effect when he was the Duke of Anjou. Though they were not openly hostile to each other politically, neither felt the slightest affection for the other on a personal level. But if she were to marry his cousin, Henri would never be able to offer Philip assistance.

"What if enemy ships should sail up the Thames?" Elizabeth asked the architect. "Can the docks be closed?"

"Not closed, Majesty. But here we have gun positions—"

Lord Howard interrupted. "The second portrait, Majesty. King Erik of Sweden."

The queen looked around, suddenly realizing one of her entourage was missing. "Where's Bess?"

Bess had slipped into the Privy Garden, looking for solitude, and was reading, completely caught up in Spenser's poetry: *So let us love, dear Love, like as we ought.* The most romantic bits she read aloud, then closed her eyes and tried to imagine someone penning such perfect phrases for her. Gentlemen wrote poems for the queen, but they weren't like these—these were less self-conscious, more unfettered, full of genuine passion. As she considered this, she began to understand the queen's loneliness. There was something empty in the attention Elizabeth received from her courtiers, gentlemen much younger than her, who, when Her Majesty was not in the room, were all too happy—relieved, even—to flirt with ladies their own age.

She closed the book, tucked it under her arm, and had begun to wander through paths lined with boxwoods cut at perfect right angles when she panicked at the sight of how high the sun had risen. She was late. She picked up her skirts and ran back inside, through the corridors of the palace, dodging crowds of lesser petitioners who were waiting, hoping, to gain access to the queen.

As she reached the doors of the Presence Chamber, she saw the gentleman who'd been with the puddle man, outside, the other day. Beside him were two fierce-looking foreigners, whose dark skin and rough features made all those around them seem sickly pale. Then, despite herself, she gasped. There was the puddle man, looking much more handsome than before, trying—futilely, she thought—to persuade the doorkeeper to let him in to see the queen.

"Just look aside for a moment," Raleigh said, pressing a coin into the man's hand.

The doorkeeper pocketed the coin but did not step

aside. "You'll have to see the Controller of the Household, sir." Beyond the open doors to the inner rooms stood the Controller, a portly man surrounded by persons no less eager than Raleigh to see Elizabeth.

"Christ in heaven. I had less trouble than this boarding a Spanish ship of the line," Raleigh said, and Bess nearly laughed. This man was witty and appealing; the queen would like him. The doorkeeper moved, but to let her through, not him. Bess flashed the stranger her most stunning smile as she passed, her heart fluttering.

RALEIGH WATCHED THE GIRL—A vision of blond loveliness—go by. "Tell the queen the New World is beating at her door," he called out, but she gave no sign that she'd heard him and he was left stuck on the wrong side of the doors. He leaned back on his heels, frustrated.

"I told you, sir," Calley said.

"Don't be so quick to lose faith." He tried to think of another way to convince the doorkeeper to admit him without further waiting but found himself wholly distracted by the memory of the girl's upturned lips. It tugged at his chest, surprising him. He would not have thought anything could distract him from his purpose, even for a moment. She'd been carrying a book; he wondered what it was.

Elizabeth shook her head as Bess rushed into the room and curtsied, low and elegant, before her. "Late again, Bess."

"I beg Your Majesty's forgiveness," the girl said, cheeks warm. Elizabeth wondered if it was from running or from embarrassment. The pearls dangling from her ears quivered as the crimson flush traveled from her chest all the way to the roots of her blond hair.

"Given. Once."

Bess sighed, her relief evident. "The puddle man is outside, Majesty."

"Is he?" Her interest was piqued. He was showing a pleasing persistence and might prove more interesting than most of the gentlemen at court. Or, more important, than any of the princes fighting for her hand in marriage. She took Bess's arm and turned her to the row of portraits. "Come. You must help me evaluate my suitors. Who do you have for me, Lord Howard, aside from the Frenchman with the foul breath?"

Howard was standing next to the third easel, his jaw clenched. "The Archduke Charles of Austria, Majesty. The younger brother of Maximilian II."

"He's rather sweet," Elizabeth said, studying the image of a handsome young man with reddish-brown hair. "More your age than mine, Bess, don't you think?"

"How old is he?" Bess asked.

"Sixteen, maybe eighteen . . . I think," Howard said.

"Would he mistake me for his mother?" the queen asked. She and Bess looked at each other and burst into laughter, their heads bent together as Walsingham stepped forward.

"An Austrian alliance would stick in Philip's throat."

"Always ready to seize the opportunity, aren't you, Moor?" The queen looked across the room at the Spanish delegation, all surly, none among them attempting to hide his displeasure at being kept waiting. "I become almost enthusiastic. Send for him," she said to Lord Howard, smiling, then turned to Bess. "I think we're done here, and I'm overdue for some amusement. Why don't you bring me the puddle man?"

The girl bobbed a curtsy and hurried to the door.

"How much longer do you think I can play this game?" the queen asked, her voice quiet as she returned to her throne with Walsingham by her side.

"Virginity is an asset that holds its value well," Walsingham said.

"Diplomatically speaking." The queen's face betrayed no emotion; her cheeks did not color; her lips did not move. But her eyes danced, just a little. She had no intention of marrying any of these men, but she had no objection to being wooed.

There was a commotion as the door opened and a motley party led by Bess and the puddle man, dressed far better than when she'd seen him last, entered the room. As soon as they'd started toward the throne, the Spanish ambassador cried out an objection and started to push his way forward, not bothering to hide the anger in his voice.

"Majesty, this man is well known to be a pirate," Don Guerau said, thrusting an angry finger at the newcomer.

"Indeed?" asked the queen, finding more than a little humor in the irritation on the Spaniard's face.

The ambassador motioned to the hampers carried by Raleigh's men. "Spanish treasure, stolen from Spanish ships. Attacked without provocation."

Silent, Raleigh knelt before Elizabeth, who gestured for him to rise. "Well, sir. Who are you?"

"Walter Raleigh, Your Majesty." His eyes lingered on hers in a most deliberate fashion.

"What is your rank?" she asked.

"A gentleman of Devon."

"What do you want?"

"Merely the honor of finding myself in the presence of my queen, whose radiant beauty is the boast and glory of the English people."

"Yes, well, here you are." Her eyes betrayed her amusement, but she kept her voice firm. She was no stranger to flattery. This man was handsome, moderately interesting, but he would have to offer something more if he hoped to gain her favor.

"I'm just returned from a voyage to the New World, Majesty. I have claimed the fertile coast in your name, and called it Virginia, in honor of our virgin queen."

"Virginia?" she asked, raising her eyebrows. "And if I

marry? Will you change the name to Conjugia?" The royal entourage laughed with more sincerity than usual.

Raleigh showed no sign of distraction, keeping his focus on her. "I ask for your gracious permission, Majesty, to return to the New World with your royal warrant, to found a colony under the laws and protections of England."

"A colony?" she asked.

"A permanent settlement, Majesty, that will bring riches and honor to our country, that will expand our empire, that will—"

"Yes, I understand," she said, looking at the natives standing stiff in their European clothes. "Who are they?"

"Americans, Majesty. They long to be your newest subjects." He motioned to Calley, who led Wanchese and Manteo forward.

"Have they no ruler of their own?" Elizabeth asked.

"None to match England's queen. Manteo is the chief of his people, yet even he wants to be led by you." Raleigh's smile was winning. Elizabeth studied the two men, fascinated, then held out her hand. Manteo took it, shaking it as the courtiers around them gasped, but Elizabeth accepted the courtesy with grace.

"What do they think of your plans for colonization?" she asked.

Raleigh came closer to her. "I have never encountered natives more friendly or helpful. They're already learning English and realize there is much we can teach them. A colony would benefit them as much as us."

"A very optimistic view, Mr. Raleigh."

"An explorer must be optimistic, Majesty, or he'd never leave the safety of home."

She liked the brightness in his eyes when he spoke. "These gentlemen are welcome," she said. "See that they're treated well."

Raleigh motioned to Calley, who ushered Manteo and Wanchese out of the room. "I also come bearing gifts for Your Majesty, from the New World." He nodded to his men, who brought forward the hampers as Don Guerau interrupted again.

"The fruits of piracy, Majesty. The true property of the realm of Spain."

"Let's see, shall we?" the queen asked, then turned to Raleigh. "What do you bring me?"

"Mud and leaves," Raleigh said.

"Mud and leaves?" she asked, a hint of laughter in her voice. The courtiers tittered, but Elizabeth's attention fell to Walsingham, who was watching the exchange with an interest that suggested concerns beyond the spoils of the New World. He would want her to be careful about antagonizing Philip and Spain.

Raleigh bent down and opened the first basket. Don Guerau peered inside, suspicion covering his face, then scowled, drawing more muffled laughter from the audience. Raleigh pulled a dirty-looking vegetable out and waved it in front of the ambassador before turning to the queen. "*Pa-*

tata, Majesty. You eat it. Very nourishing." He pulled the lid off the second container and drew out a brown leaf as the Spaniard continued to track his every move. "*Tobacco*. You breathe its smoke. Very stimulating."

The courtiers were no longer concealing their amusement and their laughter—all of it directed at the ambassador—grew too loud to ignore. Don Guerau drew himself up, a vision of angry pride, deep creases on his brow, lips pulled down. His own king would never allow such a spectacle at court.

"Forgive me, Majesty. I find the air has become stale. I am sensitive to the smell of open sewers." A glare at Raleigh, a bow for the queen, and he led his countrymen from the room. Elizabeth covered her mouth with her hand, unable to stop herself from laughing. She'd never thought entertainment could stem from anything involving Don Guerau. Raleigh was growing more and more attractive.

"Continue," Elizabeth said as soon as the Spaniards were gone.

Now Raleigh was smiling, broadly, eyes full of life. He gestured for his men to bring forward the third basket, then drew out of it a gold coin and handed it to the queen.

"Gold. You spend it," he said. "Very satisfying."

She pulled her eyebrows together, all traces of humor gone from her face as she took the coin and examined the image of Philip on its obverse.

"Courtesy of a Spanish ship that found itself unable to complete its journey," Raleigh said.

She dropped the coin back into the basket. "I can't accept the proceeds of piracy, Mr. Raleigh."

"Philip of Spain is no friend of England, Majesty. The more gold I take from him, the safer you will be," Raleigh said. "He balks when English ships refuse to respect the monopoly of trade he wants wherever his flag is found. And if you did not agree with me, I doubt very much you'd have sent Francis Drake to annoy him."

Philip had stopped all English ships in Spanish ports, and it had been a paralyzing blow to trade. In response, Elizabeth had unleashed Drake, favorite hero of the seas, explorer and soldier, on her nemesis. He'd met with nothing short of spectacular success. Success that she knew—not only because of what she'd seen when Philip was in England with her sister, but because of the reports from Walsingham's spies—had made Philip furious. "Well, well." She considered the man before her. "A political pirate. A logic-chopping pirate."

"And Your Majesty's most loyal subject."

Their eyes met for too long. Yes, she liked him. It was decided.

"But not my best-dressed," the queen said. "Welcome home, Mr. Raleigh."

"Mr. Raleigh." Walsingham overtook him in an arched corridor after he'd left the Presence Chamber. "A word of advice. It amuses the queen to show you favor. You will naturally take advantage of that. But do keep in mind that even her private affairs are matters of state." He paused. "Don't ask for too much."

"You think all I want is money," Raleigh said.

"I hope all you want is money." He walked on. Raleigh watched him go, thinking about his words and realizing that he'd very much enjoyed the queen's sense of humor and quick wit. Machinating to win favor for his expeditionary plans would not be the chore he'd expected.

As Walsingham disappeared down the hall, a tight group of the queen's ladies burst out of the doors of the Privy Chamber. Their laughter bounced off the walls as light heels clattered on the stone floor. "'Mud and leaves!' I nearly died," Margaret said.

"'*Patata!* You eat it!'" Bess said.

"She liked him. I could tell."

"Well, wouldn't you?" Bess asked. Raleigh smiled, listening to their banter, pleased to hear himself spoken of in such a favorable way. He walked straight toward them, and both girls fell quiet when they saw him in their path. He met their curtsies with a debonair bow, his eyes singling out Bess.

"I'm glad to have the opportunity to thank you," he said. "Without your help, I'd still be in outer darkness."

"I did very little, sir." Bess flushed as she spoke. "You'd already caught the queen's eye."

"Then I thank you for the very little," he said. Their eyes danced together for a moment before Margaret pulled Bess away from him. The ladies continued on, their chatter and laughter growing more enthusiastic as the distance between them and Raleigh grew.

It was a pretty scene. But in the shadows, a man watched, taking careful note of the flirtation, knowing that Walsingham would want a full report. If he hurried, he might hear news from other agents, agents whose jobs entailed gathering information far more compelling than that of the romantic hopes of ladies-in-waiting.

THE QUEEN HAD BEEN strumming her lute and singing for more than an hour, but Bess was not paying attention. She'd returned to the poetry she'd been forced to abandon that afternoon. The music room in Elizabeth's private quarters was full of admiring courtiers, so it seemed safe to assume that no one would notice her, tucked into a window seat, staying quiet. She wasn't actually focused on the poems, retreating instead far into her head.

"What are you reading, Bess?"

"Spenser, Majesty," she replied, startled to see the queen standing in front of her. She hadn't even noticed the music had stopped.

"Well I must complain to him about the quality of his

poems," Elizabeth said. "They're not holding your interest."

"I—"

"You're distracted, Bess. You held the book upside down for half an hour before you realized it and I know precisely why."

"Distracted, Majesty? No, I—"

The queen dropped next to her on the long bench. "It's our new friend, Raleigh. He's terribly distracting. You would deny it?"

"Raleigh? Yes—no—I wouldn't deny it. He's distracting." She loved the sound of his name, and remembered his devastating smile, his rich voice. How had he so quickly filled up the space in her head?

"We're amused by him, too, Bess. I think we shall have him back soon."

Chapter 4

"I may need you to do more," Walsingham said, handing a piece of paper to the man across from him in a forgotten room hidden deep in the hallways of Whitehall. He'd hired Thomas Phelippes as his cipher secretary, and working with him was nothing short of a pleasure. His skills as a cryptographer were unmatched in all of Europe. He was infinitely clever, motivated, and discreet. All of this was important, but it was his discretion that mattered most when it came to his latest assignment.

"I'm at your disposal," Phelippes said, taking the paper and leaning forward, resting his chin on his hand. Walsingham funneled to him all of the coded messages his agents intercepted between Mary Stuart and the men who hoped to place her on England's throne. The scheme was working flawlessly; the cipher had given the conspirators a false sense of safety. They were holding back no details, confident that their code would protect them.

By analyzing the frequency with which each character occurred in the letters, Phelippes, a brilliant linguist, shattered completely the privacy of the correspondence, providing Walsingham with a fast-growing mound of evidence against the former Scottish queen.

"The copies you've made of the original letters are flawless," Walsingham said. Phelippes not only deciphered the messages, he copied them with all the skill of a master forger. The original letters he returned to Walsingham and the copies were delivered to Mary and her friends. "We're quite certain they've raised no suspicions."

"I'm most pleased," Phelippes said. "I've been extremely careful."

"And it is much appreciated. Things are moving along quickly, but in the future, I may need you to do something more."

"Of course. Anything."

"We may need to add a postscript to some of the letters."

"A postscript?"

"Only if we're unable to persuade the devilish witch to write what we need. Her very existence is a danger to the queen."

"You need only ask." Phelippes's eyes were sunken in a face ravaged by smallpox. "My loyalty is absolute and I will do anything necessary to protect England."

Walsingham looked at the man and saw nothing but sincerity. He trusted Phelippes, not only out of instinct, but because he had checked carefully to make sure there was no reason not to. It was good to know there were some people in whom he could place absolute faith. Loyalty was a rare thing.

Mary was dangerous. His agents in Spain had been sending a steady stream of unsettling information for months. Philip would like nothing more than to have a Catholic queen on the throne of England, and Walsingham knew there were traitors in London and elsewhere willing to help the Spanish king achieve just that. He was close to being able to prove it, but he also knew there were conspirators he'd not yet found. They haunted him, stalked both his dreams and his waking hours, and he prayed for the strength and tenacity to do whatever necessary to ensure they were stopped before they could carry out their immoral mission. Nothing was more important than keeping Elizabeth safe.

On the outskirts of London, Savage was taking none of it well. He'd failed his compatriots when he ran from the armorer instead of killing him. Failed them even before he'd run, when he'd revealed his anger and raised the man's suspicions. Failed them with the horror in his eyes after Reston had dealt with the man. Now, standing alone among trees, a forest dark around him, he shivered, his face blanched as he half-mumbled, half-sang an endless prayer.

"Salve regina, mater / misericordiae, vita dulcedo et / spes nostra salve . . ."

His fellow conspirators sat nearby, close enough to watch him, but none looked at him. They stared at the fire burning before them in the clearing, its light cutting through the trees. Only a fourth man who stood, ignoring the fire, focused on Savage.

"His weakness endangers us all," Reston said, no longer dressed in his Jesuit robes, presenting the perfect picture of an ordinary Englishman. "He can't go on with us. And we can't leave him behind."

"Surely he won't take much longer." Babington watched his friend holding the gun, pointing it at nothing.

"We cannot wait," Reston said. "Who among us has the courage to show him mercy and send him to God?" Silence hung over the fire. Reston considered the men before him. He would take care of it himself, but the time had come for others to share in the blood. It would guarantee their loyalty. "Would you have him die a suicide and suffer for eternity in hell?"

Babington met his stare, nodded, and headed off through the trees. No one save Reston looked in his direction.

Reston had personally selected each man to join his mission. Babington, though young, was a true idealist, while Ramsay had an easy manner that allowed him to blend in anywhere. Francis Throckmorton, whose focus was unwavering, had connections at court. They were all fervent Catholics, all willing to die in the service of returning England to the true church, and all had been very clear as to what would happen should any of them prove less than reliable. Martyrdom never came to cowards. Savage's family history and his devotion to God had impressed Reston, and it was not often his impressions of people were wrong. He prayed God would forgive him for not recognizing the man's utter lack of strength.

"Ad te clamamus, exsulaes filii / Evae / Ad te suspiramus gementes et / flentes in hac lacrimarum valle . . ." Savage, continuing his semi-delirious chant, leaned against a tree, then stood again on his own, his glazed eyes fixed on the gun. He raised it to his temple, then lowered it, swaying on his feet, looking up as Babington approached him.

"Make your peace with God," Babington said, taking the pistol from his hand. Savage stood still, his eyes suddenly clear. He stepped back from his friend.

"No! Don't kill me. I don't want to die." His limbs were trembling with such ferocity it looked as if he were convulsing. Babington swallowed hard and raised the gun, then paused, breathed deeply, and pointed it to the ground.

Now Reston started to pray, his voice strong. *"Si ambulam in medio umbrae / mortis, non timebo mala—"* The others gathered behind him and joined in, reciting together the words of the psalm. As Babington added his voice to theirs, he began to weep.

"Quoniam tu mecum es, Domine. / Virga tua et baculus tuus, ipsa / me consolata sunt—"

As if fortified by the holy words, Babington raised the

pistol, continuing to pray aloud as tears streamed down his face. He squeezed the trigger.

Savage would tremble no more.

Francis Walsingham, his mind still full of conspiracies, returned from Whitehall to a house that was not as grand as his position and proximity to the queen would have led one to expect. He spent freely when he wanted to and was a frequent patron of musicians. But the bulk of his fortune went toward funding the work of gathering intelligence, work essential to ensure the queen's safety, a matter that concerned him only slightly less than the glory of God. There was nothing more dangerous than belief in security; no one was ever secure.

He'd established an extensive network of agents throughout the world and regularly received updates from twelve locations in France, nine in Germany, four each in Italy and Spain, three in the Low Countries. Constantinople, Tripoli, and Tangiers were within his reach. He'd found no court or household that did not contain at least one person ready to gossip. Solid news often required payment, but Walsingham never balked at that. Personal fortune was nothing compared to the security of the realm.

Not that his wife always agreed.

The walls of his study in Seething Lane were lined with oak cases that hardly began to provide enough space for his books. With shelves overflowing, volumes were stacked on every surface, heaped on the floor, on chairs. His desk was covered with papers, letters, maps, and codebooks—everything he needed for the work that consumed him.

The door opened and Walsingham looked up from his desk, the frown on his face disappearing as he recognized his visitor and lifted his arms to embrace him. "You look terrible. Don't they feed you in Paris?" He pushed back to get a better look at his younger brother. "How are your studies? Learned the secrets of the universe yet?"

William smiled, tired but at ease. "Not yet."

"You study theology and these are dangerous times to be questioning the ways of God. You must take care of yourself."

"My needs are simple."

"But are they safe?"

"I do what I must, brother. You know that."

"You'll dine with us?" Walsingham asked. "You'll lodge with us?" Two women, mother and daughter, all smiles and dimples and beautiful gowns entered the room.

"William!" Mary exclaimed, tumbling into her uncle's arms.

"Look at you. All grown up."

"I'm twenty, you know," she said, eyes bright with innocence.

Walsingham's wife, Ursula, came forward, raising an eyebrow at her brother-in-law, an unasked question on her lips. "William. This is a pleasure."

"I've been away too long, ma'am," he said.

Mary took his arm and started to lead him out of the room. "You come with me, William. There's much we need to discuss."

As they left, heads bent together, laughter following them out the door, Ursula met her husband's eye. "He's not still a student, is he?" Walsingham did not answer but took her arm and steered her down the winding staircase toward the sound of his daughter's voice.

Mary and William were already comfortably ensconced in the hall, he sitting by the fire, she at the small table that held her virginals. She started to play, first a bright fantasia by William Byrd, showing off her quick fingers, then cycled through a stack of popular songs. Her voice was a sweet delight, and her father would have been content to sit quietly listening to it.

"Have you spoken to the queen?" Ursula asked. They were sitting across the room, by a long table.

"I speak to her daily," Walsingham replied. "You know that. Have you suddenly decided to be impressed?"

She did not respond to his attempt at levity. "You know what I mean. You've done enough." The urgency in her tone distressed him; he did not like to cause her grief. "No man could do more."

"I can't leave court yet. The queen needs me." His eyes were dull, his shoulders had begun to stoop, and his movements were not as fluid as they had once been. But his voice was strong, authoritative. Much though he adored Ursula, he would never abandon Elizabeth.

Anger flashed in her eyes and he fought the urge to be irritated. "So you're to die in a harness like a packhorse, are you?" she asked. "And for what?"

Walsingham bit back a sarcastic remark and fumbled for something to say that would not be incendiary. "I like to think of myself as a thoroughbred, not a packhorse. Have you such a low opinion of me?"

"Francis." His wife took his hand. "You are the best man there is. I've never doubted that." He leaned over and kissed her cheek as Mary came toward them, her arm in William's.

"So, William," Walsingham said, his voice deliberately light. "What do they say in Paris of the Pope's call for holy war?"

"Many welcome it." William hovered next to the table, his eyes not meeting his brother's. He tugged at the ruffled collar, stiff around his neck.

"Sit, sit," Ursula urged.

"Here by me, William," Mary said.

"I don't understand why we must all hate each other," Ursula said, her steady gaze resting on her brother-in-law.

"Truth will always hate falsehood, ma'am," William said, sitting next to Mary.

"Trouble comes when two sides both think they hold the truth." Walsingham watched his brother carefully, trying to read his reaction.

"But only one of them can be right."

"There are few issues more divisive than religion," Walsingham said. "I'm glad to find myself on the side fighting for the truth."

"How can you be certain you're in possession of the truth?" William asked.

"I know it with all my heart. There's not a shade of doubt in me. I've devoted my life to protecting it."

"Why do we have to talk about war?" Mary asked, petulant. "You must have news, William. Are you married yet?"

Her uncle smiled. "Not yet."

"Then we must find you a nice sensible English wife," Mary said.

"No, no." William shook his head. "I won't be staying long. I must go back to my studies."

His brother looked at him and spoke in measured tones. "Not too soon, I hope. Every man deserves a rest."

"Listen to him!" Ursula said, casting her eyes to the ceiling. "When did you last rest, I'd like to know?" She leaned toward William. "He won't listen to me. Not a thought for his health. You tell him; he's your brother. He'll die at his desk, out of sheer selfishness."

Servants came in, carrying steaming platters of chicken boiled with leeks, mackerel with gooseberry compote, and artichokes baked with sherry and dates. Delicious smells filled the room as footmen poured wine.

"There are worse ways to go, madam," William said, filling his plate.

"I cannot agree," Ursula said. "No man should have to be so consumed with the business of state. He thinks nothing of us, only England."

"My dear." Walsingham gave her a tired smile. "No one doubts my adoration for you."

"I should hope not," his wife said. "But I'd like to ensure many more years of it, Francis. You'll do us no good dead."

"Quite," William agreed, applying himself with unusual enthusiasm to the food before him.

"I'm afraid your concern should focus more on my dear brother. It is he who risks running himself senseless."

"My studies are not so ferocious," William said.

"No?" Walsingham asked. "I wonder if that is so."

William swallowed an enormous bite of mackerel. "What about you, Mary? Why aren't you yet married?"

Mary's silvery laughter delighted anyone who heard it. "I've exacting taste, sir, and have not yet met someone who meets my standards. Perhaps you could suggest a candidate?"

Walsingham sat back as his brother set himself to the task of playing matchmaker. His focus was obviously deliberate, and Walsingham knew there was little chance he'd learn anything further about the religious implications of William's studies unless he turned to covert methods of information gathering.

Luckily, the covert was his specialty.

Chapter 5

The Presence Chamber was packed more tightly than usual, none of the courtiers wanting to miss the newest suitor, Archduke Charles of Austria, vying for the queen's hand in marriage. Gossips claimed he could be the last, not because she would fall in love with him—no one expected that—but because she had reached an age at which she would no longer be able to bear children. No children meant no heir, and the lack of an heir would leave England in a precarious position. But the queen had always scoffed at issues of succession. God, she insisted, would take care of the matter, but the courtiers were skeptical. Not that any of them would dare admit that to her. Silence fell across the room as Elizabeth entered.

Stunning and terrifying, sumptuously gowned in the finest cream-colored velvet encrusted in jewels, she kept her ladies close to her while Walsingham stayed discreetly in the background. A tall, stiff collar fashioned from starched lace rose from the bodice of her dress as amethysts and canary diamonds set in gold draped her neck and hung from her ears. Her hands, covered with rings, rested unmoving on the arms of her throne as she sat, her entire person radiating regal grace as a shy, slight, shaking sixteen-year-old stepped forward to make a formal declaration of love.

It was difficult not to be bored in these situations. Early in her reign, Elizabeth had been amused—vaguely—by proposals of marriage and the suits of foreign princes. Her feelings on marriage had always been ambiguous at best, and her suitors were rarely appealing. She did not need a husband to gain a throne, did not want a man to guide her rule. Taking a spouse would degrade her power and having a child might kill her. Frankly, it seemed a bad business in which she stood to lose everything dear to her while gaining nothing.

Except love, of course. She might gain love, and that was the only thing that might entice her to marry. Not ordinary love, though: it would have to be passionate, enduring, consuming, and never compromise her role as queen. Was there a man alive capable of giving such a thing? She was skeptical even as she hoped. Not even her darling, darling Robert had succeeded in giving her all she needed, and she could not even imagine a man better than he.

Despite his faults.

There were always faults.

Today, however, she had no concern for love. She had to pay attention to the boy in front of her, and a quick glance to the side of the room brought a smile to the royal lips. The Austrian ambassador was quietly mouthing the words to him as he spoke. She felt a stab of sympathy and focused on the awkward speech.

"Your Majesty's beauty is dazzling to my eyes," Charles von Habsburg said, voice unsteady, tension evident on his not-unattractive, youthful face. "I see before me perfection in human form. I am overwhelmed. I am conquered. I die. Only your love, great Elizabeth, can restore me to life."

The courtiers who filled the room with their brightly colored finery smiled, keeping their laughter silent. Not so thoughtful were the members of the Spanish delegation, who made no effort to hide their sneers. But the queen maintained her composure, looking at the boy with serious eyes, sympathizing with his nerves, knowing full well that it was not a simple thing to have to tend in public to business that ought to be entirely personal. When he had finished his speech, she gave him her hand to kiss.

"Your Highness does me great honor. Shall we go to dinner? It should prove almost as restorative as my love." She slipped her arm through his and together they led the court through the mazelike corridors of Whitehall, their way lit by thousands of candles. "We shall dine in comfort," Elizabeth said, leaning toward him. "But this palace could use a true banqueting hall. I ought to have one built. Are you interested in architecture?"

"I—I hardly know." His voice was still shaking. He was

a decent-looking man, far too young for her, but his nervousness touched her and she would not see him tortured by the court. For a moment, she considered him for Bess. They would make a good match. But she was not yet quite ready to give up her friend to matrimony.

Soon they were seated at an ornately dressed high table, on which stood an enormous castle sculpted out of sugar, flags depicting the arms of Elizabeth and the archduke flying from its towers. Musicians and tumblers waited on one side of the room, ready to entertain the guests, and there were more people in the room watching the party, eager to see the spectacle, than had been invited to eat. Among the observers was Walter Raleigh, who had taken care to dress in the latest court fashion, as handsome a man as had ever been in the palace. Bess Throckmorton lowered her eyes as she met his smile with one of her own. Elizabeth, watching, raised an eyebrow.

"So tell me, Mr. Raleigh, in your sea battles—how do you sink an enemy ship?" one of the courtiers asked, hardly able to take her eyes off him. "You shoot holes in its sides, I suppose."

"No, ma'am," Raleigh replied. "A sunk ship is of no value. The object is to capture and command."

"And how do you do that?" she asked.

"Surprise. Speed." He leaned closer. "Irresistible violence." Calley, next to his captain, rolled his eyes.

Elizabeth could just make out their voices and was fully distracted by watching Raleigh flirt. She appreciated a man who could hold the attention of so many ladies, whose handsome features were matched with a quick wit and a ready smile. A not inconsiderable length of time passed before she realized that she was ignoring the archduke, who was picking at a dish of spiced rabbit.

"I think you're not as accustomed as I am to eating in public. I have a secret." She lowered her voice. "I pretend there's a pane of glass—*eine Glasscheibe*—between me and them." With an elegant flair, she moved one hand before her face, indicating an imaginary pane of glass, noticing as she did this that Bess, who had stepped away from her, was still watching Raleigh. Amused, she beckoned for the girl, who came to her at once.

"He interests me." Her voice was low. "Talk to him."

"Him, my lady?" Bess asked, moving her head slightly to indicate the man in question.

"Him." She was not being subtle in the least; it was obvious she was staring at Raleigh. Bess nodded, tugged her lip, blushing as she set off to speak to him. Elizabeth took a bite of chicken with rice and almonds and turned back to the archduke. "His Highness is tired after his journey."

Shy beyond measure, frozen, he stared ahead, trembling, and Elizabeth could practically imagine him trying and rejecting responses to her simple statement. She did not rush him, gave no indication that he was taking too long. At last he spoke. "No man can be tired in the presence of so lovely a queen."

"You play the game very well, my young friend." Breaking a piece of crust off a mushroom pasty, she spoke softly in German, hoping that would make him more comfortable. "But don't you find it hard sometimes not to laugh?"

His eyes flew wide, then relaxed as Elizabeth shot him a conspiratorial smile. "I'm too afraid to laugh," he said.

"Why be afraid? We poor princes can only do our duty, and hope for the best."

"You're very wise, madam." Grateful relief flowed from him, and he scooped up a large bite of rabbit from his plate, then drained his glass of wine before applying himself to the rest of the meal and accepting a heaping serving of golden steamed custard seasoned with saffron.

AT THE FAR END of the room, Bess faced Raleigh. "The pirate is not too bored by the vanities of the court, I hope," Bess said, eyes sparkling, lips drawn in a winsome smile.

"A simple sailor, dazzled by the bright lights," he replied, the ladies surrounding him all but sighing over his every word. He showed no displeasure at their attention but gave no indication of disappointment when Bess drew him farther away.

"If you can bring yourself to leave the dazzle of the bright lights for a moment—"

"Drawn away by the brightest light of all," he said, catching her gaze, holding it.

Bess's cheeks flushed dark as claret as he spoke, and her reply came too quick. "That can only mean the queen."

"I don't presume to raise my eyes so high." He turned to the queen, and with a wicked smile across his face, bowed low.

"It seems you've presumed after all," Bess said.

He stepped closer to her. "It seems you're determined to think the worst of me."

"Tell me what it is you really want." Her voice was soft, intimate, bright.

"What every man wants. Money. Fame. Love."

"In that order?" she asked, looking up at him through golden eyelashes.

"Each leads to the next," he said. "The money will buy and equip ships for a return voyage to the New World. The success of my infant colony there will make me famous. The fame will bring me love."

"It seems rather a long way round," Bess said.

"There are benefits along the way. It is something, after all, to take a blank on the map and build there a shining city." There could be no question of his enthusiasm; his entire body radiated it, pulsing with energy.

"Which you will no doubt name after yourself." Her tone teased.

He smiled. "No doubt."

Bess paused, considered. "Well, then. I am answered."

"May I ask a question in return?"

"Of course," she said.

"How am I to win the queen's favor?"

"Why should I tell you that, sir?" She could not help flirting with him; he was far too charming, far too good-looking.

"I've little enough to offer, I know. But whatever I have to give—ask, and it's yours."

Bess thought for a moment, studying his face, the creases between his brows as he looked intently back at her. "My advice to you is say what you mean to say as plainly as possible. All men flatter the queen in the hope of advancement. Pay her the compliment of truth." She offered her hand, which he took and kissed at a pace so leisurely that it made all the skin on her body crave more of his touch.

"I don't even know your name," he said.

"Elizabeth Throckmorton."

"A second Elizabeth."

"Everyone calls me Bess." She looked away, suddenly self-conscious, curtsied to him and returned to the queen. Halfway there, she turned back. He was staring after her.

"WHAT HAVE YOU TO tell me, Bess?" the queen asked when she reached the high table. "What have you learned about our puddle man?"

"He is . . . magnetic, Majesty. Mesmerizing. Handsome." She smiled, leaned close and whispered. "His breath is the sweetest I've smelled."

"High praise," Elizabeth said. "I'm pleased." She would encourage the girl's friendship with him, if only to keep him close. She had not expected to find him so fascinating. The court had long been needing a new bright spot, and she was delighted to have found someone who might be a suitable candidate.

Bess slipped back into her seat, and the queen, who had long since finished eating, whispered in German to the archduke, who smiled in response. Silence fell over the room as she rose from her chair. "His Highness the archduke informs me that my charms overwhelm him. He will retire to his private quarters to rest."

A swell of laughter filled the room and drew looks of disgust from Don Guerau. The archduke swallowed the last bite of custard, stood, and bowed solemnly to the queen before departing with his entourage. When he was gone, Elizabeth motioned for Walsingham.

"He's a sweet boy," she said. "I don't want him hurt by your schemes. You're to send him home."

"Majesty—"

She did not let Walsingham interrupt. "Find another way to annoy Philip."

❧

Elizabeth's private rooms in Whitehall surrounded an elegant atrium, a space into which only those closest to her were allowed. Here she had a small measure of privacy to pursue her passions. Her love of books stretched back to her youth, when they offered solace to a girl whose fortunes changed as often as her father's wives. As an adult, even in the face of the demands of government duties, she tried to spend three hours every day reading and kept a ready stock of books in her library. Across the atrium was the music room, where she could play her lute or virginals, sing, and write music.

There was a small room in which the queen could pray, and a large room to store her enormous wardrobe, rumored to consist of no fewer than two thousand dresses, many of which were New Year's gifts from her admiring—and wealthy—subjects. She had exacting taste and insisted on being the most spectacularly dressed woman in any room, a feat not difficult when fortune provided no obstacle. The finest fabrics, laces, and embroidery were at her disposal, and she insisted on silk stockings rather than cloth. Her selection of jewelry—from ropes of pearls to strings of diamonds—was unmatched.

To enhance her complexion, scarred, though not badly, by a bout of smallpox, Elizabeth turned to ceruse, a foundation made from lead and vinegar, which brightened her skin. A wash of egg white across the cheeks would give a smooth finish and a hint of vermilion on the lips would complete her toilette with stunning results that were mimicked by her courtiers, always eager to imitate the queen.

It pleased her to see them copy her, although lately she'd begun to notice a disparity between herself and her ladies. They were so much younger, and no matter how spectacular she was, she could only hide her increasingly fragile skin and dulling complexion for so long. It was impossible to compete with youth.

This angered her. On occasion she'd considered having only ladies older than herself around her. But she found them too dull. She had no doubt she could bewitch any man—who could resist her, the virgin queen? No mortal man. Not when an alliance with her could bring him the world.

Which was precisely the problem. Who could love her and not want her to bring him the world? She considered Raleigh. He was a man who already had the world, or at least parts of it—and she had begun to wonder, tentatively, cautiously, if he might have something worth offering to her.

"I suspect him of being a professional charmer," she said to Bess, who was seated next to her in her bedchamber, closing the book she'd been reading to the queen. "Am I right?"

"He certainly is charming, my lady," Bess replied, a delicate hand flying to her cheek. Elizabeth felt like a girl, sharing whispered confidences with a friend.

"There are duller professions," Elizabeth said. "And what is it that he hopes to gain by his charms?"

"He hopes for glory in his New World. He dreams of

building a shining city." There was a revealing eagerness in Bess's voice, an eagerness shared by the queen, though she would not admit it to her lady-in-waiting.

"You'd think it would be enough for a man to discover the place, but already he wants more. That's the drawback of America. There's so much of it." She stopped, watched Bess, saw the hint of color creeping up her face, the way she bit her lip. "You like him, don't you?"

"If it pleases you."

"Ah, well. It's refreshing to meet a man who looks to a world beyond the court. Let him come again." And she knew, as she said the words, that she would be looking for him every time the door opened, every time someone was announced. She welcomed the feeling, happy for the distraction, because when she was not thinking of him, she would be forced to deal with the increasing difficulties caused by her Scottish cousin.

THE ONLY REAL SOLACE Mary Stuart had from the moment she'd made the mistake of fleeing to England was the ladies that surrounded her. She depended upon them. They were her only company, and she valued each of them, even her servants, as friends, despite the fact that at times they were absolutely incorrigible. At the moment, the laundress was crying so hard that her words were all but impossible to make out, but Mary tried not to be frustrated with her.

"Tell me again," she said, handing her a handkerchief.

"Dismissed." She'd finally managed a coherent word, and this success seemed to soothe her enough that she found her voice. "I've been dismissed."

"Dismissed?" Mary was holding Geddon in her arms and had been stroking the little dog's soft fur, but stopped. "On whose orders?" More crying. "You really must stop sniveling." The laundress had fallen into complete incoherence again. Mary turned to Annette. "Who dismissed her?"

"The warden, my lady," Annette said.

"The warden? *My* warden?" She spat the words, then flew around at the sound of the door opening, her tone changing entirely as Sir Amyas Paulet entered the room. She walked to him, eyes soft, her voice all teasing seduction. "So you dismiss my laundress, sir. How am I to have clean clothes? Or do you want me to go about naked?"

"That was not my motive, Majesty," Paulet said, his voice steady. "Your laundress was found to be carrying letters in her washing."

"Intimate letters," Mary said, leaning close enough to ensure he could smell her perfume. "Private letters. Love letters."

"Love letters?" The warden's eyebrows pulled together. "I was aware that you had a husband, ma'am, who, sadly, died. And a second husband, who, sadly, died."

"Yes, yes—" Mary began.

"And a third husband . . ."

Now she was irritated, her voice rough. "That's enough. Am I to have no privacy?"

"You are a queen, Majesty," Paulet said. "A queen belongs to her people."

"Then why am I not being treated like a queen? Why does Elizabeth not answer my letters? Why does she not come to see me? Why does she hate me?"

"The queen does not hate you." She saw a measured kindness in his eyes.

"Has she told you so? Have you met her?" Mary asked.

"I have had that honor, Majesty."

"What's she like? Is she beautiful?" Jealousy laced her words as she wondered—no, doubted—that Elizabeth could be more attractive than she.

"She has a queenly air."

"So do I have a queenly air," Mary said, forcing herself to flirt again. "But, more than that, some have said I am beautiful." Beautiful, yes, but that was not all for which she was known. Her voice—with its lovely Scottish lilt—charmed, and her wit and passion had drawn many a man to her, including more than one of her jailers. Yet it infuriated her to have to flirt with such men, so far beneath her station. It was untenable that a queen should come to this. She tried to bury the anger she felt building deep inside her.

"In the words of the poet, *Fair child of beauty, glorious lamp of love—*"

She could stand it no longer. "Damn your poet!"

Paulet recoiled. Mary closed her eyes, composed herself, knowing it would be politic to keep the warden under her spell. With a graceful hand, she waved away her servants.

"My friend, forgive me." She was sweetness, the silver rays of the moon, beauty itself. "You are my friend, aren't you?"

"I am your servant, ma'am, and your admirer." How easily he was captivated.

"I shall send no more letters. I shall stay here quietly, in my prison. With you." Lingering eyes made promises she would never keep and reminded her that Elizabeth had brought her to this low station. It was unforgivable. There were times when Mary thought there could be a peaceful resolution to her troubles, but she was beginning to believe that less and less.

When Paulet left her, she knelt on the hard floor and pressed her hands together, offering first a prayer of thanks for the friends who were helping her and, second, one that God would speed the resolution of her plans. She did not pray for mercy for her cousin. Elizabeth would have to take care of herself.

Chapter 6

Darkness poured through the leaded-glass windows of the Privy Chamber, but the queen was enraptured and would stand no interruption as her new favorite regaled her with stories of his adventures. Raleigh was animated, his eyes sweeping the room as he spoke, but his attention lingered on two women: Elizabeth and Bess, though every time he looked too long at the latter, he abruptly turned away and focused on the queen. It had taken Elizabeth fewer than ten minutes to notice this, but it did not trouble her. Bess knew her place. No harm could come from letting her flirt.

As the hour grew late, she heard a few mumbled complaints among courtiers wondering when they would be allowed to eat. This, of course, served only to make her delay even longer, but she did not see how they could mind. Raleigh's story was entrancing, his personality magnetic. A meal could wait.

"It begins with a journey. You must cross an ocean. Can you imagine—can you feel—what it is to cross an ocean?" He paused as his audience nodded, enthralled. "For weeks there is nothing but the horizon. All round you. Perfect and empty. Your ship is small—tiny—a speck in such immensity. You live with fear, in the grip of fear—fear of storms, fear of sickness on board, fear of the immensity. What if you never escape? How can you escape? There's nowhere to go. So you must drive your fear down, deep into your belly, and study your charts, and watch your compass, and pray for a fair wind—and hope." His gaze locked onto the queen's. "Pure naked fragile hope, when all your senses scream at you, *Lost! Lost!* Imagine it. Day after day, staring west, the rising sun on your back, the setting sun in your eyes, hoping, hoping—"

Sir Christopher Hatton slowly crossed to Elizabeth. "Majesty, the court is waiting."

"Let them wait, Lids."

"I think—"

"They can wait." Her voice was sharp with irritation and she considered that Lids, her old favorite, might be jealous of his replacement. Her tone was all softness as she turned back to her explorer. "Go on, Mr. Raleigh. You were hoping."

Hatton looked as if he would say something else, but she shot a glare at him and he bowed and left, a frown on his face.

Raleigh continued, looking straight at Elizabeth. He

seemed as undaunted by her steady stare as she was by his, and noticing this brought a pleasant sensation to her chest and a smile that stretched her face and crinkled her eyes. "At first it's no more than a haze on the horizon, the ghost of a haze, the pure line corrupted," he said. "But clouds do that, and storms. So you watch, you watch."

She could have listened to him for an eternity. His voice was mesmerizing. But eventually, she too became hungry. "I think, Mr. Raleigh, we will have to eat." She took his hand—a hand stronger and more calloused than any she'd felt—and led him to supper, ignoring the rules of precedence.

The meal, which had been ready for more than an hour, had suffered from waiting. Not knowing when the queen and her party would arrive, the servants had not sent the food back to the kitchens, and as a result, the soup was cold, the meat's sauces had congealed.

"I can't remember when I've had such a satisfying meal," Raleigh said.

"You're the only one not complaining about everything being cold." Elizabeth motioned for more wine.

"Your courtiers have not lived aboard a ship. They know not how bad food can be."

"Yet you prefer your ship to the palace?"

"Not for comfort, of course," he said, taking a second plate of mutton.

"The company, then? You prefer sailors to queens?"

"If, Majesty, all my time in London was spent with you,

I'd have a very different view of city life. The lure of the sea, though, surpasses any desire for comfort or activity. There's nothing like it."

"Perhaps not," she said. "But I think we can amuse you sufficiently to entice you to stay with us some time."

"At the moment, I'm perfectly content where I am." The tentative connection between them had grown with every sentence that day, and Elizabeth found that she could not recall feeling more comfortable with another gentleman. Raleigh leaned close when he talked to her, and more than once reached for her hand or arm during the meal. His touch thrilled her.

"Come," she said, standing when she was done with her ruined food. "I want to dance with you."

The rest of the court, though still complaining about the food, now rushed to finish eating before the queen made her way out of the room. The procession following her grew smaller as it reached her private quarters, where musicians had gathered in the atrium to play.

He was her partner; she'd allow him no one else. She might have, just to watch his elegant movements, but rejected the idea as soon as she felt their bodies move together, then apart, then close again, their rhythm mimicking the motion of Raleigh's ship on the sea. She had no intention of sharing this pleasure with anyone else.

"You have not finished your story," she said as they danced. "You left off watching. Continue."

"Watching, yes." He smiled down at her. "You were listening to me, weren't you?"

"You have all my attention."

"You see a smudge, a shadow on the far water," he said. "For a day, for another day, the stain slowly spreads along the horizon, and takes form—until on the third day you let yourself believe. You dare to whisper the word—*land*!"

"I would love to feel the thrill of it," she said, her breath coming harder.

"Land. Life. Resurrection," Raleigh said, pulling Elizabeth close, the air between them crackling. "The true adventure. Coming out of the vast unknown, out of the immensity, into safe harbor at last. That—that—is the New World."

Bess, who had been watching them from one of the arches lining the atrium, idly took the hand offered her by a courtier who wanted her for the next dance. She could tell the queen was captivated and that Raleigh was something far more than content—she'd noticed an intensity in his eyes that made them look a darker shade of green than usual. When the music began, Bess faltered over steps that should have been familiar.

Jealousy had tripped her, and she chastised herself for her feelings. Raleigh could never be hers. She needed to be more careful about guarding her heart.

Two days later, the Austrian delegation gathered in the Presence Chamber to hear the queen's official response to the Archduke Charles's proposal. No one expected she would marry him, yet the room was so crowded as to be virtually impassable; everyone wanted to see the form her rejection would take. The suitor himself had to fight his way to the front, where he stood, face pale, nervous, waiting for his would-be bride. Around him, the atmosphere vacillated like a stormy wind, the mood varying from group to group: a sour sort of giddiness from the Spaniards, sighing resignation from a cohort of young ladies who admired the handsome man, urgent anxiety from courtiers and ministers concerned with the issue of succession.

Elizabeth entered, resplendent in an elaborate gown of white velvet, her red hair full of pearls and diamonds, and sat on her throne. She'd made no secret of her fondness for the young man since his arrival at court. She treated him with a careful, dignified respect, and had laughed with him on more than one occasion, but she picked up no hint of passion from him, which was a relief.

Not that she'd expected to. He was hardly more than a boy. Years ago she would have been able to captivate him in an instant, to lure him to her side and keep him there, hoping he would earn a kiss. But longed-for kisses, whether given or merely anticipated, had, in her past, led only to increasingly urgent proposals. It was much easier to reject someone who didn't want her, except to fulfill the duties he owed his country. She sighed. This was less painful in many regards. All regards, really, save the uncomfortable recognition that her looks no longer drew every man in the room to her.

Charles was approaching the throne. She flashed him a smile as he knelt before her. It was a smile full of promise and understanding and friendship, tender and sweet, and was quickly replaced by another expression, this one coolly regal.

"The queen does not have a private life," she said, her eyes steady, watching him. "The queen lives for her people. You will therefore forgive me, sire, if after much thought and prayer I decline your offer of marriage."

The archduke did his best to conceal relief, but his body went from stiff and awkward to relaxed. Tension flew from his face. Hands that had been clenched released. He turned to the Austrian ambassador, speaking his native tongue. "Can I go home now?"

Elizabeth inclined her head, freezing the smile desperate to form. "Go home, my friend," she answered him in German. "Don't be in a hurry to grow old. Youth is so very precious."

He bowed his head. "Your beauty does not end with your face." He spoke quietly but with more confidence than she'd heard before in his voice, and the earnest sincerity of his tone nearly brought tears to her eyes. She quickly composed herself.

"You will make someone an excellent husband," she said, standing and giving him her arm. Murmurs of approval, scorn, and disappointment hummed through the crowd as it parted to allow the couple to pass, but she cared not for any of it. She'd successfully dodged the marriage question for the moment and as soon as the archduke left court—preparations for his departure had already begun—she would have more time for Raleigh. And the thought of that set her heart to soar.

Bess, lost in a sea of ladies, left the room well behind Elizabeth. As she rushed to catch up to her mistress, she saw Raleigh walking toward her. Her heart pounded, and nerves made her worry that she wouldn't find coherent words to say, but she went straight to him. "Are you satisfied with the queen's favor?" she asked, blue eyes meeting his, then looking away, then back up to him.

"She listened as if she understood me. I was talking about solitude and infinite emptiness. Some of the things she said—I thought never to hear from a queen."

"And did you expect to dance with the queen?" A teasing lilt filled her voice. He was easy to talk to. Too easy. "A few more dances and you'll be a duke. Then I shall expect some gratitude."

Their eyes met, lingered. They smiled, and the heat she saw in his scared her.

"We should walk," she said, starting to turn away. "We've fallen awfully far behind."

"What do you want?" he asked, coming closer to her.

"I'm not sure." Her voice was a bare whisper and their gazes held steady, a delicious tension filling the space around them. She was excited and terrified and looked around to make sure the queen couldn't see them. Elizabeth was nowhere near, but Bess felt a pang of guilt at flirting with her mistress's favorite.

"I expect I'll think of something." His voice was deep, and the sound of it sent color to saturate her cheeks and chest.

"I'll look forward to it," she said and rushed after the queen, wanting to get away before the feelings he inspired took up residence in her heart.

ELIZABETH DID NOT DAWDLE over formal good-byes. She sent the Austrian delegation off as quickly as possible but made a point of bidding farewell to each of them individually, kissing the archduke on the cheek as he turned to leave the palace. When they were gone, she paused for a moment, relishing the knowledge that she had at least half an hour before Walsingham and the Privy Council would need her again. She turned and searched the courtiers, looking for a head of curly hair.

"Mr. Raleigh!" she called when she'd spotted him, standing back from the crowd not far from Bess.

He came to her at once, bowing low. "Majesty. How can I serve you?"

She laughed. "You can stand up, first. Take my arm and come with me." He followed her orders, and she ducked through a door, pulling him outside. "It's lovely to escape the court, don't you think?"

"Lovely to find myself in such company when I escape the court," he said. "I'm flattered."

"You should be." They made their way down a gravel path, along a row of espaliered fruit trees, past a sundial and a fountain. "It's not often that a gentleman so quickly wins my favor."

"Nor is it often that a lady is so fast to capture mine."

Elizabeth raised an eyebrow and laughed as the path turned, taking them into a knot garden. The air around them was filled with the sweet scent of herbs: santolina and marjoram, hyssop and thyme. "You are not like other men at court. You offer something more, something different. I like your immensities. Your ocean is an image of eternity, I think. Such great spaces make us small. Do we discover the New World, Mr. Raleigh, or does the New World discover us?"

"You speak like a true explorer," he said.

"I like you, Mr. Raleigh."

"And I like you."

"Your directness is refreshing. I think I shall call you Water," she said, her blood like hot lead in her chest. A flash of fear came on its heels, but she ignored it. "And you know, of course, that when I like a man, I reward him."

"I have heard that."

"And what have you to say about it?"

"Reward my mission, Majesty, not me."

"Why not you?" His response confused her, and she did not like the feeling; it put her immediately on guard.

"Leave me free to like you in return. That can be my reward."

"I don't understand." She pulled back, her eyes clouding, the lines on her face hard.

"So long as you are a benefactor, I cannot cease being a beggar," he said. "I've not come here for personal gain."

"I know not what you mean."

"I think it must be difficult for so great a queen to know the simple pleasure of being liked for herself."

She stared, shocked, after he finished speaking. He'd come uncomfortably close to the truth, and discomforts, no matter how small, were not something she ever intended to bear well. In fact, she generally made a point of not bearing them at all. How dare he draw attention to the difficulties of her situation? This was a liberty he should not have taken.

He should have fallen to his knees and thanked her. She could return to the palace and in an instant find a hundred men who would beg to find themselves in his position, who would know better than to point out her most private vulnerability. Not, she suspected, that any of them would have the means—or inclination—to discover it. And it was this thought, more than any other, that troubled and frightened her.

"Now you become dull," she said. She turned and walked away from him, kicking at a patch of violet-colored sweet William as she went. Once she was far enough away that it was unlikely he could still see her, she started to run, hot tears stinging her cheeks. She ran until she could no longer catch her breath and then dropped onto a stone bench. She would have to be more careful with this man. It would be dangerous to allow him closer to her heart.

WHITEHALL WAS QUIETER AT night than Bess had expected. Darker, too. Though she didn't know why she'd had any faith in her expectations. She'd never before found herself in the corridors of the palace in the middle of the night, and certainly hadn't ever embarked on a clandestine mission. She was carrying her shoes, knowing that their heels would be startlingly loud on stone floors and, as she made her way silently through the hallways, stayed close to the walls.

It seemed the safest approach, though when she thought about it, if a guard or anyone else came upon her, she wouldn't, in fact, be able to disappear into the stone. Soon after she'd left her room she'd heard something: creaking wood, a turning handle, the rustle of skirts. She'd stopped, afraid that she'd been discovered, and pulled the hood of her cloak down low over her face. Flattening herself against the wall had made her feel slightly less visible, and rational or not, she had decided that walls were her best protection.

She'd waited, but no one came forward to confront her, so she continued on, haunted by the unsettling feeling that someone had been watching her. When she left the grounds of the palace—having slipped on her shoes as soon as she'd come outside—she entered a world wholly unfamiliar to her. She could not risk taking one of the royal boats; someone would notice her, and she'd have to pay off the boatman. He'd thought of this, of course, and arranged for a boat, rowed by an anonymous man who'd never know she'd come from Whitehall, to be waiting for her at a nearby dock.

The man did not speak to her during their short journey. When they stopped, she consulted the note in her hand before setting off on dark streets littered with the city's homeless, their sleeping bodies obstacles in her path. He'd promised she would not be harmed, that the neighborhood was not as dangerous as it looked, and that his colleagues would be watching from the shadows, ready to intervene if anyone gave her trouble.

If she'd stopped to fully consider what she was doing, terror would have paralyzed her. So instead, she imagined that Raleigh was with her. First she'd pretended that they'd stumbled upon each other as she left Whitehall. A pleasant coincidence. Then, feeling more bold, she imagined that he'd followed her deliberately, and she distracted herself from the horrors of the dark by inventing both sides of the conversation they would have had were they together. He might comment on the stars; she might ask him about the poetry he wrote. Whatever the topic, she never doubted that their talk would be easy, effortless, perfectly satisfying. A feeling of sweet comfort burned through her.

And then she caught herself wondering if thoughts of her ever danced in his mind. She tried to stop, but it was too late. Thinking this way was useless, and there was an immediate sinking in her heart. He was the queen's favorite and no one at court doubted the feeling was entirely mutual. He adored Elizabeth. How could he not? The queen was everything—beauty and power—and could satisfy his every desire. Bess had nothing to offer but herself.

This stung, hurting all the way to her teeth, and she was angry at herself, both for wanting him and for ruining her fantasy by letting reality creep into it. She imagined his eyes and made them smile as he would turn to her and say . . . say what? It would no longer work. She could not conjure up his side of their hypothetical conversation, and the streets seemed darker, unsafe.

Her thoughts turned as bleak as the winding alleys, and she began considering the man who'd asked her to come to him, her cousin, Francis Throckmorton. They'd played together often as children, but he'd always been more serious than she, and as they grew older, they saw each other less frequently.

Francis had never found a position at court. He'd stayed quietly in the country, holed up at his father's estate after leaving Oxford three years ago. Now he said he needed her, summoned her to come in the middle of the night—bad signs—but family loyalty kept her from refusing to see him. As she reached the house, she looked at the message again, wanting to be certain she was in the right place before knocking on the worn wooden door.

"Bess! God bless you." Francis opened the door and ushered her into a modest room. The furnishings were rough, not to the standard he or Bess had grown up expecting.

"What are you doing here, Francis? You must be more careful." She held out his note. "What if this had fallen into the wrong hands?" She held the paper over the flame of a candle, dropping the charred remains as the heat started to burn her fingers.

"Can't I send a note to my own cousin?"

"Your father's a notorious Papist—"

"He's an old man!"

"—and a defender of Mary Stuart—"

"That's my father, not me." He could say that, but any connection to Mary, no matter how tenuous, was dangerous, and Bess knew full well that he was an ardent Catholic, even if he was careful about hiding the fact. "Listen to me, Bess. I know England's changed. The old faith is gone, and it's not coming back. If I'm to have any kind of future, I have to change, too." He looked at her, eyes pleading. "I want a place at court."

"They'll never trust you at court, Francis. You know that."

"Why not? Everyone at court has a Papist somewhere in his family. Just as you have."

"The queen knows I'm loyal." As she said this, her

thoughts flew back to Raleigh. There was nothing loyal about her feelings for him, feelings she had no right to, not when she knew that he belonged to the queen.

"What if she finds out you've met me here tonight?"

"Is that a threat, Francis?" Beads of sweat clung to her forehead, worry showing itself on her pursed lips. She was behaving recklessly, coming here like this. The queen trusted her, but she knew well how quickly royal opinion could change and shuddered at the thought of finding herself exiled from court.

"Help me find favor with the queen. Then I'll not be a danger to you."

Her voice was low, quavering. "You must want this very much."

"So you will?" he asked.

"I don't know. Give me a little time to think."

By morning, Bess had nearly convinced herself to embrace the idea of Francis coming to court. He might reform, renounce his father's Papist ways. He could be a charming man when he tried—the queen might find him amusing. But even as she thought these things, something tugged at her, something that would not let her believe her cousin was being forthright with her, that his reasons for wanting to join the court weren't altogether innocent.

Margaret and several other ladies had come for her. They were all due to sit with the queen, who was planning to play a new piece she'd composed for the virginals. As they walked toward the music room, she considered what Francis's motivations might be, and anxiety consumed her again. Inordinate numbers of rumors made their way through court—whispers of conspiracy, of terrible men bent on killing the queen and putting that Scots woman on the throne—but surely Francis would not embroil himself in anything that dramatic. It was not, however, unrealistic to worry that he might be seeking a position from which he could gather information—could he be a spy?

She smiled at the thought, thinking of her cousin who, as a child, couldn't even hide well during a simple game. Margaret tugged on her sleeve, and she looked up to see Walsingham standing directly in front of them. They all curtsied, Bess feeling the burn of his eyes on her the whole time.

"I can't believe he bothered to pay us the slightest attention," Margaret said once he'd gone.

"He's never been particularly social," another of the ladies, Jane, said. "He did have words with all of us who were here when he'd begun to suspect Lettice Knollys was having an affair with Robert Dudley, but I'd hardly call that social." The affair—and the couple's secret marriage—had been discovered at least six years ago, but the queen still refused to receive the Countess of Leicester.

"Well, you can see why the queen was so upset," Margaret said. "She's always loved him. And Lettice Knollys bears a striking resemblance to her—I think she has wigs made specially to look like the queen's. She even mimics Elizabeth's walk. It's revolting. And if anything, I think it's unsavory for Leicester to choose a wife that looks so much like the woman everyone knows he loves."

"They were foolish to try to trick her," Jane said. "But I suppose it all worked out in the end. I've heard the countess's wardrobe very nearly rivals the queen's. And she was treated like royalty when they lived in the Netherlands."

Bess had been holding her breath. "I'm surprised Walsingham felt any of this was a matter worthy of his consideration."

"He's got a hand in everything, Bess. Don't make the mistake of thinking that by not speaking to us he's not taking notice of what we do." Jane turned back to Margaret. "You know, I had been very close to Lettice before her marriage . . ."

Bess stopped listening and was again consumed with worry. If Walsingham discovered she'd left the palace in the middle of the night, he would tell the queen. And then what? She was sweating, the bodice of her dress itching as it grew damp, and she wished more than anything that she could disappear, spend the day in private, doing anything but waiting for Walsingham to confront her.

They'd reached the music room. Margaret and Jane took seats near the window, their heads bent together, still gossiping. Bess hung back, watching the queen and Raleigh, who were sitting close, the queen in front of the virginals, a beautifully relaxed expression on her face. She looked younger than she had in years, and Bess knew at once it was because of him, and her heart sank deeper into the mass of confusion that was becoming its permanent home.

"So am I forgiven?" Raleigh asked, and she looked down at the keyboard in front of her before she found herself too captivated by his smile.

"I wouldn't go that far," she said, beginning to play again.

"I had no intention of offending you. I thought you'd be pleased to know that I have not befriended you looking for personal rewards."

"Instead you seek rewards that will take you away from me. And you—" She stopped, not certain that she wanted to continue.

"Yes?"

"I don't need to tell you another thing," she said. "The privilege of royalty."

"I'm afraid that my words in the garden hurt you." He put his hand on top of hers, stopping the music she was playing. "You must know that I only wanted to tell you that I do—very much—desire to like you for yourself."

"You presume too much," she said, not looking at him but beginning to feel more favorably disposed to him once again. "I am a queen—that is part of me. You cannot separate it from the rest."

"But your heart is your own, is it not?"

She studied his hand on hers, debated how to respond. She wanted to trust him, to reveal her whole self, but it was too difficult, too frightening. "Tell me more about your New World."

He gave a small smile, a slight shake of his head, a hint of laughter. "You'll give away nothing, will you?"

"Virginia, Water. I want to know more." She began to play again, a lively tune, something she thought would remind him of the dances they'd shared.

"The land, Majesty, is more fertile than any I've seen, and the variety of fish that can be caught off its shore staggers the imagination. The coast is not like ours—no cliffs like Dover—just sandy beach. You would find it most beautiful."

"I'm certain I would," she said. "Perhaps I should visit your colony—once it's suitably civilized. I am, after all, its ruler, am I not?"

"I shall take you there myself. Though I'm not sure you'd much like the accommodations on the *Tyger*. You might consider having something more regal built."

"Don't tease me, Water," the queen said, falling fully back into the informality that had grown between them. She had forgiven him, couldn't resist him, didn't even want to try. "There's nothing I'd like to do more."

"So why don't you?"

She gave him a calculated smile and her long, slender fingers stopped, resting on the keyboard. "All right, then. I will." He blinked but did not speak, surprise registering on every inch of his face. Elizabeth laughed. "You liar! You don't want me on your ship at all."

She looked up and saw Bess hanging in the doorway, not joining Margaret and Jane, who'd come into the room earlier. "Take Bess if you like," she said, motioning to the girl. "Not me. Would you like to go to sea, Bess?"

Bess stepped into the room and took the seat farthest from Raleigh as he shook his head. "I'm afraid that's not possible. Women bring bad luck onboard ship."

"Oh, do they?" Elizabeth asked, incredulous. "Why is that?"

"Lock up a hundred men in a space smaller than this room, for months at a time." He leaned forward, a wicked flash in his eyes. "Men have needs. A beautiful woman like you would drive us all mad."

The queen smiled, laughed, amusement on her face. "Men have needs?" She met Raleigh's stare, then broke away, wanting to give herself a moment to decide if she wanted to initiate such intimate contact. A pause and she looked back, level and clear. "Then let them remain on land and see to their needs."

"You make remaining on land infinitely more bearable, but—" He stopped as the queen turned to Bess, interrupting him.

"Mr. Raleigh is eager to sail away to his infant colony, Bess. We must persuade him to stay a little longer, mustn't we?"

Bess said nothing, just gave a small smile and stared at

the floor. Elizabeth knew at once what was keeping her favorite lady quiet. She recognized the blush, the hesitation, the rapt attention whenever he spoke to the girl. And when he wasn't talking to her, she'd noticed that Bess would hang back, watching, something in her eyes that looked dangerously like love.

Night crept through London, rendering the streets silent again, the alleys dark, and laying bare the dangers of ordinary neighborhoods to anyone lurking in the shadows. Francis Throckmorton knew his friends would watch out for Bess, but he found himself worrying about her nonetheless. He was asking her to risk a great deal to come to him, more still should she agree to help him.

He did not feel good about deceiving her, about letting her believe he supported the queen and was ready to play Protestant. But there was no chance for him if he told her the truth. So he prayed that he'd be forgiven for lies he believed in his heart were unavoidable.

And he prayed that the dangers he faced would not stretch to his cousin.

He knew well what would happen if he were discovered—relentless torture on the rack or the scavenger's daughter and then a traitor's death. But how was a man to resist doing God's will? And if he did, would not the punishment he'd face in the afterlife be infinitely worse than anything that could be done to him on earth?

A knock startled him, pulling him from his thoughts, and he looked out the window to make sure it was she. He saw her hood, her blond hair tumbling out of it, and unbolted the door, relieved that she had decided to come to him again.

"Bess?"

But it was not his cousin. He didn't recognize the woman who left her head covered and stepped away, fading into the night. Before he could call out to her, two men burst through the door, grabbing him. He struggled, squirming to regain his freedom, flailing his arms and legs, unable to release the firm grips of his captors. In the end his ineffectual efforts gained him nothing but a single sharp blow to the head. As consciousness escaped him, he almost smiled. He was about to face every horror one could suffer on earth and hoped he was right—that they would pale in comparison to endless agony after death.

Chapter 7

William the Conqueror had built the palace at Windsor as a fortress, replete with bailey, motte, and keep, choosing for it an easily defensible site, on a hill above the Thames. Five hundred years later, it remained a safe respite for England's monarchs, a retreat to which Elizabeth frequently returned. She had more privacy here than in London, more space, and more opportunity to pursue recreation. Within the royal grounds was the Great Park, an expanse of land—thousands of acres—for hunting stag, and it was here she loved to ride when she craved the wind in her hair and the feeling of fast freedom that came with thundering hooves.

Two horses pounded over the grass, manes flying as they raced over the tree-covered grounds of the palace. Their riders, faces glowing, laughed, abandoning themselves to the breakneck speed of the moment. Elizabeth spurred her steed on as her opponent pulled in front, first by a head—

she could still catch him—then by a length—the odds were slimming—until at last she met him after he'd stopped.

"Mine!" Raleigh called.

Elizabeth shook her head, smiling, out of breath. "You have the stronger horse."

"Yours carries the lighter load." He swung to the ground and took the hand she held out, helping her dismount.

"And the better rider." She tossed her reins to him, and he tied them to a tree. "It must have been the horse."

"You'll never get me to agree," he said.

She walked forward, ahead of him, looking at the great swaths of land around her. There was nothing stunning to the view, but it was bucolic, a perfect pastoral scene. "Yes, I remember this." They'd gone the length of the Long Walk, leaving its manicured lawns and the castle hardly a dot behind them on the horizon, and from there, followed no path, racing up hills and down, through trees and next to Great Meadow Pond, coming at last to a heap of worn rocks, ancient ruins. "I used to come here when I was young."

Her childhood, though far from straightforward, had been generally happy. She'd adored her father, despite the fact that he'd executed her mother, Anne Boleyn, when Elizabeth was only two and a half years old. She couldn't remember it, of course, but when thoughts of the stories she'd heard about it did creep into her mind, late at night, when the moon fought its way through the curtains of her bed, she'd wake up and find herself unable to breathe.

Raleigh was staring at her. She'd not painted her lips vermilion that morning and they looked like pale petals, soft and parted as all hints of haughty regality drained from her face. "What has taken you so far from me?" he asked. "I can see that I've lost your attention."

"I was thinking of my mother. And my father. I remember making a book for him when I was a girl. It was full of prayers that I'd translated myself, written in my best handwriting. I embroidered the cover."

"Did he like it?"

"Yes, he did." She looked at him, narrowed her eyes and pursed her lips. "Of course he liked it. I was his daughter. And my handwriting is spectacular."

"I've seen your embroidery."

"You have?"

"I make it my business to admire your talents," he said.

"Do you?" she asked, pleased with the attention.

"I certainly do. Other than your embroidery, I've evaluated your dancing and singing, and have taken note of the fact that you're a skilled linguist. But I've not yet seen your handwriting. Perhaps you should send me a letter."

"Perhaps I will, but only if you write to me first."

"I already have," he said. "Have you not seen my verse?"

"What verse?"

"I scratched it onto a windowpane in your rooms at Whitehall. You'll have to look for it."

"What does it say?"

He grinned. "You'll have to look for it."

"On a window? How did you do it?" she asked.

He pulled a ring from his finger and handed it to her. "A diamond. They cut glass, you know. Though not very well. The method was far from efficient."

"I shall find your verse, Water." She looked at his lips, considered what it would be like to kiss them, and realized, with no small measure of satisfaction, that she *could* kiss him. They were alone. She'd almost convinced herself to lean forward just enough that he would know what she wanted when he smiled, making her feel instantly self-conscious. "Why do you smile?"

"Because you smile," he said.

"I was thinking how rarely I'm alone."

"But you're not alone," he said. "I'm here."

"I mean, alone—with one other." They were walking toward the ruins, so close together that their hands kept tangling. "I love Windsor. It's equal turns majestic and practical. Could withstand a siege. There's no place I feel more secure, more removed from danger."

"And does that give you the freedom to be simply a woman?"

"I don't know that I could ever be that. Even if, somehow, I could view myself in such a way, it's unlikely anyone else would be able to do the same. A futile effort."

"Would you allow anyone to consider you only a woman?" He searched her eyes. "Have you?"

She thought of Robert, of course, of the deep love she'd felt for him since her youth, a love still in her heart. They'd shared more than a simple passion, but even so he'd always known she was—before everything—a queen. She looked at Raleigh, at his welcoming eyes, his easy grin. "Could you see me that way?" she asked.

He hesitated longer than she would have liked. "You are my queen," he said.

"But if I weren't your queen." It was a mistake, always a mistake, to let someone this close. Her pupils grew small, her eyes hard—she could feel the resemblance to her father jumping out of her face—as she waited for a reply that did not come. "God's blood! It doesn't take much thinking about."

"Yes, it does. I'm trying to imagine you as not queen. It's hard." His voice was so earnest she could be nothing but charmed. She breathed deeply. She'd reacted too soon, been too quick to believe he was nothing more than a calculating courtier.

Her voice softened. "I'd be like, say, Bess." Their eyes met; everything blurred.

"Oh, well, if you were like Bess, I'd—" He stopped, the tension between them heavy.

She wished she could freeze the moment, never forget the way her heart raced, the way the very core of her trembled in a most delicious way. "You would, would you?"

"I'd try." His voice was ragged.

Now she would tease him. "I might not want you to. But then again . . . you are perhaps more capable than the average man. You might be . . ." She let her voice trail. "I'm not sure. What might you be?"

"Adventurous. Surprising." He threw her an undeniably wicked grin. "Talented."

She laughed, half-nervous, half-titillated, and took his hand, leading him to an ancient stone seat among the ruins. "The only surprise I find is that you're not yet married."

"I've been at sea. No marriageable young women to be found at sea." He leaned back on the hard rock. "I'm free to live and love as I please."

"And how do you please?" she asked. "To love, I mean. What sort of woman would win your heart?"

"Oh, I have all the usual requirements. She must be beautiful and clever. And, if possible, rich."

"And docile, and obedient, and have no will of her own?" She gave him a playful slap on the arm as her eyebrows shot up.

"No. I don't want a wife like a cushion."

"But you wouldn't like her to order you about."

"No, not that either," he said. "I want a lover who knows me as I am."

She considered this. "You want a friend and an equal. You want someone to share your joy when you're happy. Someone to cry with when you're sad. Someone to talk to when there's nothing to say. Someone to find by your side when you wake in the night. Someone who remembers what you once were when you've grown old." She smiled. "You see? I know all about it." She looked down, then away, drew in a deep breath and paused before releasing it. This was dangerous, this feeling rising in her, and she was not sure if she should let it go further. "There. I'm rested now."

She gave him her hand and he lifted her to her feet, but once standing, she did not let go of him, instead rested her other hand on top of his.

"Warm hand, Water," she said, hardly daring to look at him.

"Yours too." A rough whisper.

She raised her eyes to his and started to lean toward him, lips upturned, but pulled back. He raised a gentle hand to her cheek but did not touch it. They were silent, floating in a lovely warmth, neither putting expectations on the other. For the moment, this would have to be enough. But hanging in the air was an unspoken promise that someday there might be more.

"We should go," she said, taking back her hand and starting for her horse—turning away from him so that he would not guess that her heart was pounding and her soul singing. "I'll beat you this time."

She mounted first, dug in her heels, urged her steed forward but to no avail. Raleigh came up hard behind her, moving faster and faster, and she adored him as he pulled ahead of her. He was treating her as an equal, not as his queen, not letting her win, challenging her instead. The excitement was intoxicating.

❧

Bess had agreed to join the picnic, though her mood was melancholy at best. For days she'd felt paralyzed every time Walsingham passed her, jumped whenever a message was delivered—fearing it would be from Francis, that he'd want more from her when she'd decided that she would have to deny him. She had to find a better way to manage her emotions.

She heard hoofbeats thudding on the grass and turned to see two horses running at reckless speed. They slowed as they approached the courtiers, who were sitting in the shade of an enormous tree, and as they did, it became immediately obvious the queen was one of the riders. Everyone around Bess leapt to their feet, the gentlemen rushing forward to take Elizabeth's horse as she slid down from it. Raleigh was with her, but he did not join them, instead hung back from the bright array of chattering gossips vying for the queen's attention.

Bess could not help staring at him. His face was flushed with exercise, his hair disheveled, and his eyes a brighter green than the leaves above her. She looked to the queen, whose complexion was glowing in a way Bess had not seen in a long, long while, and she felt a desperate pang of jealousy; though she had no right to it. Raleigh was not hers, would never be. Ladies-in-waiting needed Elizabeth's permission to be courted, and the queen surely would not let her favorite court anyone but her royal self. Bess would have to content herself with stolen glances and bittersweet wishes; bliss she could find when she slept, and then only if he'd come to her in her dreams.

CALLEY WAS STANDING APART from the group and leaning against a tree. Raleigh grinned as he approached his first mate. "Not amused by the antics of a court picnic?" he asked.

"I don't know why I'm here. I'm not a courtier." He puffed on the pipe he was smoking. "But your friend Bess has been awfully kind to me."

"Bess?"

"Quite taken with you, I'd say."

"She's a beautiful girl," Raleigh said.

"Sweet, too."

"That she is."

"Pity you're wasting your time with the queen," Calley said.

"I'm not wasting my time."

"You are if you think you're ever going to get somewhere with her. She's not going to marry you."

"Who said I want to marry her?"

"Well . . ." Calley tapped the side of his pipe. "You said you were here to get a warrant. But it doesn't seem much of an urgent priority anymore. Not that I'm complaining, mind you. Nor are the lads—we're all happy for some time at home."

"I'll get the warrant."

"Sure you will. But what is it you really want from her?" Calley asked. "We're not getting too comfortable, are we, sir?"

WINDSOR CASTLE MAY HAVE been sturdy as a fortress, but its interior was fitted with every luxury. Tapestries woven from silk and gold hung on walls across from paintings, many of them Holbein's portraits of the royal family. Fine walnut furniture filled the rooms: tables inlaid with mother-of-pearl or topped with red marble, tall, heavy chairs with velvet seats. An enormous tester bed, its posts elaborately carved, its valance embroidered with scenes from classical mythology, stood in the queen's bedchamber.

Elizabeth and Raleigh had spent hours on horseback, and the queen had returned to her private quarters nursing aching muscles, demanding a bath. Steam clouded the Venetian mirrors that screened the tub as she submerged herself in the hot water, giving herself up to the ministrations of her ladies as they washed her. For a while, she kept her eyes closed, going over the details of her wondrous afternoon in her mind, recalling all of Raleigh's expressions, all of his words.

She considered his earlier accusation—for that's what it had felt like—that she was not appreciated for herself.

Robert, her Eyes, had appreciated her. Of that she was certain. He'd loved her before she was queen. But she could not deny that he'd wanted to be king. Water dripped down her neck, almost tickling, sending goose bumps to cover her chest and arms. She raised her knees, leaned back hard against the tub. If she hadn't been queen, she would have married him. There was no imagining such a thing, though; the monarchy was too entangled in the depths of her to be ignored or forgotten. The question she'd posed to Raleigh was impossible.

Bess was holding her hair out of the water and had begun to stroke it softly. Elizabeth opened her eyes, catching Bess's in the mirror, and the girl held her hand still, confusion painted on her face.

"No, don't stop," Elizabeth said. "I like it. What do you think, Bess? Have I never known the simple pleasure of being liked for myself?"

"I wouldn't know, my lady," Bess said, resuming her gentle caresses.

"Is anybody ever liked just for herself? Are you?" she asked, continuing to watch her in the mirror and deciding that Bess, too, was in possession of qualities that would color men's opinions. "It's unlikely. Men like you because you're pretty. And because you have the ear of the queen."

"No doubt, my lady." There was a tone in Bess's voice that Elizabeth did not like. It was too sharp, too quick, and she felt an unaccountable jealousy, wondering if Bess was in a position to experience something she could not. And as this unpleasant sensation pricked at her, she considered all the times she'd noticed the girl's affection for Raleigh.

"Him too," Elizabeth said. "He likes you because he wants my favor. You do realize that?"

"Yes, my lady," Bess said. Her voice wavered, and the rhythm of her hand stroking Elizabeth's hair grew uneven.

"And the other thing too, of course," the queen said. "But all men want that. Male desire confers no distinction." Bess said nothing, and Elizabeth straightened her legs, plunging her knees back under the water. She had not intended to be so hard on the girl. "I envy you, Bess. You're free to have what I can't have. You're my adventurer. Don't be afraid. It's all over so soon."

As she spoke the words, she was not sure what she meant. She'd never hand her Water over to Bess, not all the way. But would any harm come from letting them play, so long as she could watch them? It would be nothing more than a harmless flirtation, and it would keep him near. Wanting Raleigh for herself was so full of complications. She adored him, but what could she expect from him when she knew she could only give a parcel of herself to him? She sank lower in the tub until the water reached her chin, and wondered what it would be like to feel his hands on her body. She closed her eyes. Thoughts like this made it far too easy to lose control, but for the moment she would abandon herself to them entirely.

In London, a man bit into a cold meat pie, wished the mutton weren't so tough, and considered his plans for the evening, giving not the slightest attention to the huddled, half-naked figure trembling uncontrollably on a nearby blood-stained bench. There was no need to take notice of him, let alone guard or manacle him. The man's body was so broken he could neither protest nor resist nor even think of trying to escape, leaving his torturer to a lunch free from distraction until Francis Walsingham came through the door, nodding sharply at him as he crossed to the prisoner.

"Still nothing to tell me, Mr. Throckmorton?" Walsingham would never grow accustomed to the smells that greeted him in this room, smells of desperation and fear: excrement mingled with blood and rot. Torture was something necessary, something without which he could not prevail, but accepting this fact was not the same as embracing it.

Francis Throckmorton struggled to lift his head. "My soul will go free soon." The room was underground and poorly lit, but the darkness was not thick enough to mask the fresh splashes of sweat and blood scattered over the rack.

"You enjoyed your time in Little Ease?" Walsingham asked. The infamous cell was tiny—only four square feet—making it impossible for its occupant to either stand or sit. Throckmorton had been left there for days before being shown the rack. "I know about the Enterprise and now I need names. But if you won't help me, perhaps your father will." He motioned to the torturer, who disappeared into an adjoining room. "He's been questioned, as you have. I do have to know, you see."

English law did not allow for torture. But what went on in the bowels of the Tower was not strictly illegal. At least not in the end. Torture was conducted by royal agents given royal immunity, and though it was not something often resorted to, its frequency had increased in the face of the divisions between Protestants and Catholics, regardless of which side was in control. Religious fervor had a way of leading men to their most barbaric depths.

The torturer came back, dragging, with the help of a yeoman warder, the broken but living body of an elderly man, his joints stretched beyond the point of dislocation.

"No!" the son cried as his father looked up, eyes blank with suffering. "Enough! You want a name, I'll give you a name."

"Well?" Walsingham stepped close. Throckmorton choked, a mixture of blood and saliva catching in his throat, but managed to give Elizabeth's spymaster the information he claimed to want to know. Walsingham showed no reaction, but shock registered on the torturer's face, an expression that was both noted and remembered.

ACROSS LONDON, PAPERS BURIED the tall walnut desk behind which an impatient queen, dressed in an imposing gown of regal purple, sat in her Privy Chamber. Elizabeth sighed, lifted her eyes to the ceiling, and occasionally rubbed either her temples or the inlaid wood surface, but she would attend fully to each document Sir Christopher Hatton put before her, regardless of how much she longed to be done with her work. And she did long to be done. Water, her dear Water, was waiting for her and it was taking an unacceptable amount of energy to keep thoughts of him from consuming her mind.

"Yes, yes." Again a sigh as she read the paper. "The money must be found." The moment she signed it, Hatton replaced it with another.

"From Mary Stuart, Majesty. She asks to meet you."

"Again?" She read the letter, thinking aloud as she skimmed through it. "They say every man who meets her falls in love with her. What can be the secret of her charm, Lids?"

"A lack of all other useful occupation?" Hatton suggested, bringing a smile to his queen's face.

"So uselessness is attractive?"

"Not to me. You well know that I prefer a lady with the most serious vocation." They smiled at each other and she was glad for the memory of the time in which he had courted her. More glad, though, for the friendship that had developed afterward. They remained close, and Hatton had never married. Elizabeth took it as a token of his dedication and it never went unappreciated.

She handed the letter back to him. "Refused." He started to put something else in its place, but Elizabeth laid down her pen and held up a hand. "Enough."

Full of the excited anticipation that comes with new love, she had to force herself to walk slowly, to maintain her dignity. It wasn't easy; she didn't want to delay seeing Raleigh any longer than necessary. When she crossed through the Privy Chamber and entered her atrium, she slowed, catching her breath and moving once more with regal dignity. By the time the library door was opened for her, she was a deliberate picture of all things serene.

"Mr. Raleigh. I've kept you waiting," she said, the flush on her cheeks at odds with the rest of her calm appearance.

"I've no other business at present but to wait on you."

"I have other business. But I have been waiting too. You make things difficult."

He stepped close to her and spoke quietly, his tone intimate. "You found my verse."

"I did. *Fain would I climb, yet fear I to fall.* Did you see my reply?" she asked.

"Of course. *If thy heart fails thee, climb not at all.* Quite suggestive." He smiled, and she relished the admiration she saw in his eyes.

"You were quite right about the diamonds. Dreadfully slow."

"You were warned," he said.

"So I was."

"Majesty." Walsingham interrupted them with a low bow.

"Yes?" The queen turned to him, lips curled, irritated.

"The traitor has talked, Majesty. The traitor Throckmorton."

"Forgive me, Water," Elizabeth said, her eyes on Raleigh. "As you see, my time is not my own."

"I am most sorry," he said.

She went directly to Walsingham, and though she could barely hear the words he murmured to her, anger filled her face. "We cannot—" she began and he interrupted at once.

"I know."

"Majesty?" Raleigh asked.

"I must go," she said. She started out of the room with Walsingham, then stopped and darted back to Raleigh. She picked up his hand. "Forgive me. Will you wait for me to return?"

"There's nothing I would deny you," he said.

At the Tower, the torturer was off duty, standing in the open doorway to empty his full bladder. He heard footsteps as he unlaced his britches but wasn't in a position to turn and see who was coming. "Harry?" he asked, assuming it was his friend. "You'll never guess what I heard—"

He hardly felt the knife at his throat. One quick, hard slash and he slumped, still standing, against the wall. Walsingham's agent waited a moment, wanting to be certain he was dead. Blood trickled down, mingling with urine on the flagstones.

Chapter 8

Once Francis Throckmorton had talked, the entire mood in the palace changed. Guards on high alert lined the corridors, and archers stood on the towers, their arbalests at the ready. The gardens were empty as courtiers stayed inside, watching everyone with investigating eyes. No one was certain what exactly was happening, but every corner was rife with whispered rumors of treason and foreign threats, conspiracies and betrayal.

Elizabeth was sequestered with her Privy Councilors. She paced around the table, too agitated to sit still. "So you learned all this when you searched his house?" she asked.

"There were papers, Majesty," Walsingham said. "Naming ports that would be attacked first in a Spanish invasion—the Enterprise of England, they call it. There was also a list of Catholic sympathizers who pledged support."

"And what has been done?"

"They've all been arrested," Hatton said. "And are being questioned now."

"One thing is clear. Mary Stuart is the center of this plot. Without her, the Catholics would have no rallying point. She stands to gain more than anyone from this conspiracy. She must be held accountable." Walsingham's tone was grave.

"There is no evidence that she knew about these plans, let alone that she was taking part in them," Elizabeth said. "I will not have her arrested without proof." She noted that Walsingham and Hatton exchanged a private look, while Burghley and Howard sat motionless.

"We can confirm that the Spanish are involved, and you know Philip would put Mary on the throne if he could," Walsingham said. "You cannot let her—"

"I will deal with Spain," Elizabeth said, and stalked toward the door before anyone could respond. Her elaborate black gown, embroidered with golden thread and covered with bows, flew behind her as she swept out of the Privy Chamber into the Presence Chamber, her councilors fast on her heels. She did not sit on her throne. Instead, she went directly to the Spanish ambassador.

"What do you know of the Enterprise of England, Ambassador?" she asked.

"The Enterprise?" Don Guerau was a seasoned diplomat; she expected that lying would come easy to him. His voice dripped with friendly ease. "Forgive me, Your Majesty . . ."

"It's a plan for the invasion of my country," she said. "Two armies landing on the coasts of Sussex and—"

"Norfolk." Walsingham finished for her.

"And Norfolk," she continued, keeping her voice calm and authoritative, despite the anger coursing through her. "Mary Stuart is to be set free and placed on the English throne. I am to be assassinated. Does any of this sound familiar?"

"I know nothing of any invasion plans," Don Guerau said. "I'm afraid that your councilors have been tricked into believing nonsense."

"You may think, sir, that feigning ignorance is wise, and I pity your weak mind for not being able to conceive of something else," she said.

"No one is plotting an invasion," he insisted.

"I refer to this plan as the Enterprise of England. It should more accurately be called *la Empresa di Inglaterra*, because it's a Spanish plan. The plan of your king, my onetime brother-in-law, a man who schemed to marry me after my sister's death, to attack my country."

"Attack?" the ambassador asked. Now he was angry—she saw it in his flushed cheeks, the rushed way he spat out his words. "It is my country that is under attack! Your pirates attack our merchant ships daily. Do you think we don't know where their orders come from? The whole world knows that pirates sail up the Thames all the way to the royal bed."

Elizabeth turned on him, her eyes narrow, lips firm, shoulders straight, furious. No one would have dared stand before her father and say such a thing, nor before any male king. Yet she, a woman, could be shamed in front of her court for daring to give her heart to a man?

"You will leave my presence, sir! Go back to Spain." She stepped toward him, her hand raised as if she would strike him. "Tell Philip that I don't fear him, or his priests, or his armies. Tell him if he wants to shake his little fist at us, we're ready to give him such a bite he'll wish he'd kept his hands in his pockets."

Don Guerau pulled himself up tall, full of pride and contempt. "You see a leaf fall, and you think you know which way the wind blows. But a wind is coming, madam, that will sweep away your pride." He bowed and left, but the queen's words blazed after him.

"I too can command the wind, sir," she yelled. "I have a hurricane in me that will strip Spain bare, if you dare to test me!" Shivering with rage, she turned around, coming to face Raleigh, whose creased brow and tight lips irritated her further. He looked as if he were about to scold her.

"What are you staring at? Lower your eyes. I am the queen." She marched past him without a further glance. She did not mean to hurt him, but she had to look strong now, not to appear under his influence in the slightest. Men were too fallible, too weak. She'd been flirting when she should have been paying closer attention to Spain. She should not have allowed such distractions to take her focus away from the lover that would never disappoint her: England.

❧

RALEIGH WATCHED HER GO, pain chilling his heart and shooting through his veins. So much of him adored her, but her temper, her unpredictable nature, her need for absolute control without criticism tugged at him. His shining city would forever remain a dream if he stayed at court. He might willingly abandon it—if she would offer all of herself in return—and together they could search for new dreams. But he knew she would never give such a thing even the slightest serious consideration. He looked at the ceiling and weighed his options, pretending there *were* options. He already knew what he must do.

❧

IN SPAIN, PHILIP'S REGRET at the loss of the forests diminished as he breathed in the clean smell of freshly cut timber. Immense stacks of it stretched in every direction, and the noise of saws and hammers, instead of a cacophony, sounded like a harmonious chorus of angels heralding the raising of skeletons of enormous ships. With the completion of these new vessels, his fleet—the largest ever at one hundred and thirty—would soon be ready for its divine mission, its crusade.

But not all the news he heard was good. Elizabeth's cagey spymaster, the heretic Walsingham, had made a damning discovery, and Philip's minister, his face all serious lines, lowered his head before the king as he reported what had happened to Throckmorton.

"It can't be denied that we've lost the advantage of surprise. A large part of our plans has come into their hands."

"The Jesuit is still at liberty?" the king asked. A breeze carried the salty tang of the sea to him, the scent mingling with that of the wood.

"We understand so, Majesty."

Philip had absolute faith in Reston, whose devotion to the work of God matched his own. "He knows his business. We've lost nothing."

"Of course, Majesty," the minister replied, keeping pace with the king.

"Reston understands what is at stake, how crucial his work is. Everything we are doing is in the service of God. We must defeat the English and bring their people back to the Church. I do not desire to be the ruler of heretics."

Philip continued to walk, analyzing the progress of his shipbuilders. As their monarch passed, workmen dropped their tools and knelt before him. But Philip did not crave their obeisance. "Tell the carpenters to go on working. No one is to stop for me. The fleet must be ready to sail in a month."

The minister cringed. "Impossible, Majesty."

"If this is God's work, God will make it possible."

"Only a miracle—"

"A miracle then," Philip said. God would not abandon his most holy son. "Let it be done."

❧

ELIZABETH WAS PACING AGAIN, circling the desk in her private study. She did not think she ought to have to deal with one more problem. Was it not enough that she was managing the daily work of the country, engaging in diplomatic relations, and addressing the Spanish threat? Now she was to contend with personal matters as well?

Raleigh's letter had arrived more than an hour ago, and she had been unsettled, disturbingly so, since reading it. A host of unwelcome emotions consumed her: jealousy, disappointment, anger. But worst was the feeling that she should have known better, that she should have been more careful to protect her heart, that she'd allowed for this to be possible. As much as she wanted to despise him, hatred was not something to which she could bring herself. Not when it concerned him.

She had no intention of giving him what he wanted and knew that she'd have to do something to soften the blow. Give him something else. A pain had started in the back of her neck, and she cursed the stiff collar that made it impossible for her to rub the right spot. It always came down to this, playing queen for men she adored. She wanted to shower them with good things, wanted to bring them joy, but her generosity only led them to expect more and more until they decided that nothing short of being king would make them happy. And when she couldn't—wouldn't—

give them that, she would be the one left heartbroken. She'd wanted to keep Raleigh separate from these trappings, but perhaps that was not possible for a queen.

Still pacing, holding the paper in her hand, she waited for him to arrive. She heard his voice in the atrium, was irritated by the sound of her ladies' laughter as they vied for his attention, and willed upon herself composure. He would see nothing but a serene monarch. She would guard all her private emotions, give him what she must, and hope that her heart would not come out scarred. The door opened and he entered. She held up the letter.

"You ask permission to go," Elizabeth said.

She could see at once that he was full of angry frustration. It was evident in his tense voice, stiff posture. "Just give me my warrant," he said. "There's nothing else for me here. At sea I know what I'm to do, I know the risks, I know the rewards. Here—" He stopped, threw up his arms.

"But you're quite wrong. You are needed here. I have decided to appoint you captain of my personal guard."

"Captain of your—"

A strange sensation flashed through her, an inkling suspicion that he was not sufficiently grateful. She did not want to be angry with him, so she gave him no time to speak. "Kneel," she commanded in her firmest voice. He obeyed but did not look at her, and the omission cut. She tapped him on the shoulder with her hand. "Rise, Sir Walter Raleigh."

Again he followed her command but kept his eyes on

the ground, and she found herself unwilling to continue hiding her emotions.

"Why are you staring at your boots?" she asked, voice full of knives. "Any other man would be shouting out the news for all to hear." He would not look at her; he'd turned away. She fought the urge to force him back around and slap him. "Now you stare at the wall. Am I so hideous that you can't even look me in the face?"

He said nothing for a painful moment, leaving her to listen only to the rhythm of her racing heart. At last, he turned back, stepped toward her, met her eyes. "Why do you talk like a fool when you're anything but a fool?"

"Talk like a fool!" She threw the words, laced with venom, at him. "Please teach me better." Her eyes flashed and he paused. She looked away, afraid if she did not, she would lose herself in his stare.

"I asked Bess once to advise me how to win your favor. She said, 'Pay her the compliment of the truth.' I have done that."

"Bess gives good advice," she said, looking back at him. "My favor is won."

"But you have not paid me the compliment of the truth."

"Is a knighthood not enough? A royal appointment? How much more favor do you want?" She knew the answer. There was no point listening to him any further. She turned, ready to leave the room.

But his voice took on a gentle intensity that stopped her. "All you have."

"And what do you offer in return?" Her tone was flip, but she could feel all her sympathy returning to him, the small beginnings of a hope that he was not like the rest, that he wanted her for her.

"All I have." He could not have stunned her further if he'd struck her. Her heart pounded; she grew warm and was so taken aback she could hardly trust herself to speak.

"My friend, forgive me," she said, taking his hand. "I'm a vain and foolish woman. At court it's all a game. I like to be admired. I require it. I grow accustomed to it. But it's all nothing. You come here as if from another world, and I . . ." She gave him a smile so filled with emotion it seemed to make her lips swell. "You have real adventures; you go where the maps end. I would follow you there if I could, believe me."

"You're the queen. You may do as you wish."

"Never. How can you say so? This palace is my prison. If I were to escape—if I were to fly to that place where I—where I could give you all I have, and all I am—" Her voice trembled with emotion. "Believe me, sir, I don't cut up my heart and give it by halves. You would have all of me. You would possess me, and the queen, and all England."

A soft tenderness crept into his words as he reached his hand to her cheek. "I don't want the queen. I don't want England."

"I am all three. My own indivisible trinity."

Love, admiration, every good thing passed between

them, their eyes locked in a moment both wanted to stretch to eternity. She felt a crack in her soul and for just a second wondered if she ought to give herself to him, to bring him fully into her world, to trust that he would not disappoint her. Not yet. But maybe, eventually, soon.

"The storm clouds are gathering, my friend," she said, bringing her hand up to rest on his. "Please don't leave me now."

Chapter 9

The summer heat was raging, and a rotten stench hung heavy over London, but there was no smell strong enough, no blazing sun hot enough to keep the people away from watching the queen's justice being served. The paid seats in the makeshift galley were full, and every other inch of space around Tyburn Tree was filled with people swarming to view the day's public executions. The Tree was notorious, a permanent gallows in the west of London, shaped like a triangle and large enough to hang twenty-four unfortunate souls at one time.

Today's audience would be treated to more than the usual hangings. Today there was a traitor among the criminals. A traitor who would be hanged, cut down before he was dead, then disemboweled—his entrails shown to him before they were burned—and finally, his body would be quartered, the bloody remains displayed in prominent locations throughout the city, a not-so-gentle reminder that loyalty to the crown was preferable to the alternative.

Francis Throckmorton showed no visible response to the noose being tightened around his neck as the crowd bayed. Torture had destroyed his body, left his face a bloodied mess, but he held his head high, ready for death.

God was waiting for him.

He feared nothing, only prayed.

Lord have mercy on the soul of Your servant, who gives his life for Your eternal truth . . .

The cart upon which he stood pulled away, and he dropped, his body flailing, but his neck did not break. It was not supposed to. The executioners let him swing for a while, fighting for his breath, then cut him down, ready to continue their work.

The crowd, drunk on bloodlust, roared, ready to see the traitor meet his grisly fate.

NOT FAR FROM TYBURN, in a candlelit room hidden in a secret cellar, Throckmorton's co-conspirators knelt, Reston leading them in prayer. "May he enter heaven as a soldier returns home victorious from war—"

Babington alone did not lower his head, instead stared straight ahead, eyes unfocused, Reston's words burning until at last he could stand it no longer. "Why don't we strike? What's he dying for? Is this part of your plan?"

Reston looked up and stared, silent, at Babington, who

lowered his head, cowed by the measured intensity of Reston's burning gaze.

The Jesuit continued his prayer.

"Lord, be with us as the end approaches. We will not fail in our duty. We look beyond death, to eternity."

RALEIGH STOOD ON THE deck of his ship, docked not far from the shadow of St. Nicholas' Church, where every sailor stopped to hear mass and pray for a safe journey before taking to the seas. Work on the *Tyger* was nearly finished. It was as if the patron saint of sailors had taken special interest in the vessel, which soon would be seaworthy again. She'd required only minor repairs, maintenance really, and the work had progressed without hindrance or delay. Less certain, however, was how soon her captain would be ready—willing? allowed?—to leave England.

Part of him wanted to go at once, to get as far from Elizabeth's bewitching and frustrating charms as possible—the part of him that accepted the fact she would never really be his. She wanted to possess him but would not give him the same in return. The thought of being without her made him want to stay for eternity, content to play her game, confident that in time he could push her further than today she would think possible. But even as he considered the possibility, he dismissed it as ridiculous, bringing himself once again to the position of knowing he ought to go, and the whole cycle would begin again.

There was more, though. Hidden in his depths was

something altogether different, something that tugged at him whenever he thought of leaving. A secret smile and forbidden thoughts. Bess. He'd had to consciously stop from letting her fill every space in his brain and had done a good job of it, difficult though it was. It was necessary. In ordinary circumstances, he'd be openly courting her. But he could hardly do that when he was entangled emotionally with the queen.

Yet he could not erase Bess entirely, nor could he bear the thought of not seeing her again. Her eyes, her lips, the smell of flowers and musk that surrounded her. She was like a dream, and to allow himself to fully consider her bright wit and ready smile was to court nothing but danger. So he kept her buried, did his best to ignore the spot in his heart full of her.

"Lose you, Captain?" Calley asked. "I told you three times you've got a visitor." A wry dip in his first mate's smile spurred Raleigh to follow his glance to the dock, where he saw Bess. His heart leapt, then fell, and he felt angry, knowing that there could be only one reason for her coming to him.

"The queen's ordered you to see me, I take it," he said, meeting her as she climbed aboard the deck. "I'm seeing to my ship's repairs, nothing more. You may tell her I won't sail without her leave."

"You think everything I do and say is at the queen's command?"

"No. But I think the queen has sent you."

"Well, so she has." Her voice was stronger, the soft lilt to which he'd become happily accustomed in their previous conversations gone. "I am her servant. Of course I obey her commands. She has the power of life and death over me. I prefer life to death. That may not be particularly brave and adventurous, but that is how I am."

He stepped forward, surprised, taken aback by her outburst, eyes warm with concern. "Has the queen been unkind to you?"

"No, no. The queen is kindness itself." She turned away but not before he saw a welling of tears in eyes the color of the open sea. "A man was hanged today. A traitor. I knew him well. He was my cousin. He died because I gave information. Information to prove my loyalty. Because I was afraid."

He reached for her, raised his arm to touch her, comfort her, but stopped himself, not sure if she would welcome the gesture. "That's necessity. That's the world we live in."

"Would you have betrayed your cousin for your life?"

He did not hesitate. "Yes. And worse. We're mortal, Bess. We're sinners. We all come short of the glory of God. Even the queen who sent you to me."

"Even the queen." She turned to face him, a tear falling down her cheek.

"There now." A husky whisper. He could not keep from touching her any longer. Rough hands wiped the tear, then stroked her face.

"That's how the queen touches me," she said.

"She loves you very much." He took her face in both his hands and she looked up, meeting his eyes, and he no longer was in any doubt of her feelings for him. She took his hand from her face, moved it to her lips and kissed it, never moving her eyes from his. His breath caught as she kissed it again, this time bringing the tip of his thumb into her mouth. He drew her into his arms and kissed her, tentatively only for an instant, then eagerly, greedily, all his passion released at last.

When they stopped, they both pulled back, looking at each other with a combination of longing and confusion. "We shouldn't do this," she said.

"No. Of course not." He kissed her again, quickly, lips hardly brushing hers.

"The queen—"

"I know. To continue would be madness," he said, finding that he no longer had room in his head for such practical thoughts, knowing with a commanding clarity he would not have thought possible only five minutes earlier that their union was inevitable. "But then I've never had much patience for cowards."

"Our lives would be forever complicated. We—"

"We would be risking everything."

"Yes. And I don't know . . ." She stopped and closed her eyes, then kissed him fiercely. She tasted like cinnamon. "Could it be worth it? To risk so much?"

"Maybe."

"It would be smarter to be safe," she said. "I should go back to the palace, never see you again."

"But you will see me again. And when you do, you'll still want this, as will I."

"I never thought I could want something illicit. Something so at odds with the queen's wishes."

"Easy words until now." He touched her face. "Don't return to Whitehall. Come with me instead."

"It's madness."

"Yes." He smiled, rested his forehead on hers. "A delicious madness."

Her kiss told him she knew exactly what to do.

THEY'D BEEN CAREFUL TO draw no attention to themselves as they made their way from the ship to Raleigh's house on the Strand. It rose, magnificent, from the river and would have been more than acceptable to an exacting prince, though in fact it had been built for a bishop some two hundred years earlier. But Catholic bishops were not needed in Protestant England, and after the Bishopric of Durham was dissolved, the palatial Durham House eventually fell to the possession of Elizabeth, and she kept it to herself until she decided to bestow it upon Raleigh.

He and Bess slipped through the gatehouse and into a grand courtyard. He took her by the hand into the hall, through lengthy winding corridors and up a stone staircase to apartments overlooking the river. Putting his arm around her waist, he led her to his bedchamber and closed the door behind them, kissing her, hungry to explore every inch of her mouth, her neck, more. He did not pause even to close the curtains on windows overlooking Whitehall and Westminster.

Calloused fingers traced her breasts through soft brocade and she sighed, throwing her arms around his neck and pulling him closer. He'd already begun to unfasten her bodice when he stopped to pick her up and carry her the few remaining steps to the tall walnut bed. Then, putting her down with tender arms, he lowered himself on top of her, and she whispered for him to be gentle no more.

Deceit was everywhere in England.

This particular brand of it had been exercised often enough over the course of months and months to come down to a precise—and necessary—science. Without it, Mary Stuart would be wholly incapable of sending or receiving private correspondence, a situation that would be unthinkable.

Two dray horses pulled the brewer's wagon, its paint long since peeled away, across the ancient bridge over the moat and pulled up by the gates, the beer barrels stacked in back sloshing against the restraints holding them in place. Burton, the brewer, a big, ugly man, stared ahead, looking perfectly bored, vaguely congenial. It was an art, and he had mastered it. Ramsay, Robert Reston's man, sat next to him, offering a silent prayer that they would not be discovered.

"Morning," Burton called to the guard. He wiped sweat off his forehead with a fat hand, leaving behind a grimy smudge. "Another filthy day on God's stinking earth."

"Morning to you," the guard replied as he and a second sentry stepped forward. They meticulously searched the cargo, the space under it, every crevice of the wagon. This part always brought a tense hardness to Ramsay's stomach. He'd often catch himself holding his breath until they were waved through, and this only made him worry more that they'd be caught. He needed to learn how to mimic Burton's easy apathy.

But as always, the guards finished in short order, and soon he and Burton were rolling the caskets through a trap door, down a chute, into the cellar of the manor house. The barrels were heavy. Ramsay started to sweat as he fell into the rhythm of unloading the wagon. This was the part of their work that he liked the best, the part when his confidence returned.

"Have you met that Scots woman?" he asked one of the guards who stood, observing them. "Bad assignment to draw, being near her."

"Eh." The guard spat into the grass. "Never see her. They don't let her out much."

"I don't like that she's even in England." Ramsay leaned forward, enjoying himself. "Or that she's alive."

"Maybe she won't be for long," the guard said.

"Really? What do you hear?" He swung another barrel from the wagon and into the chute.

The guard shrugged. "She was lucky the queen didn't accuse her in that Throckmorton business. But who's to say Elizabeth won't change her mind?"

Good. Nothing new. Ramsay smiled. "Pray for it!" He

and Burton continued their work, heaving barrels until the wagon was empty.

"Last cask!" Burton called.

INSIDE THE BASEMENT, THE cellar man took each barrel as it came through the trap door and emptied the beer into large open vats, then threw the empty casks on a fire.

"Nothing but beer. Satisfied?" The cellar man tossed a wry smile at the guard.

UPSTAIRS, ANNETTE PAUSED BEFORE the door, waiting for a guard to unlock it. She chatted with him, unhurried, even smiled at him. But once the door was closed behind her, she abandoned any pretense of calm, hurrying through the apartments, calling for Mary Stuart as she removed crumpled papers from her undergarments and handed them to her eager mistress.

Taking them, Mary crossed herself and sat at her table. She devoured the contents of the missive as quickly as she could, but deciphering the code always took more time than she would have liked. At last, she looked up, rapturous, at Annette. "The gentlemen are ready. It will be soon now."

This was the news for which she'd longed, for which she'd begged on her knees for divine intervention. She'd been devastated when Throckmorton was discovered, fearing that it meant the end of her hopes. But tragic though the loss of Throckmorton had been, in the end it was only a slight disruption. Reston had sent word that it was all final. Elizabeth would be assassinated. Philip would send help from Spain and release her from this prison. At last there were firm plans—plans that were ready to be set in motion. There would be no more disappointments. She would be free to rule, to return England to the true faith. God would rejoice.

"Blessed Mother of God pray for us!" the maid said, careful to keep her voice low.

"Bring me pen and paper, Annette. They wait on my reply. Hurry, now, hurry!"

❧

SOUTHWEST LONDON WAS QUIET. John Dee had been standing on the flat roof of his riverside house in Mortlake to study the night sky, looking at the moon through a sextant, when he was distracted by the hiss and splash of an approaching barge. He was a mathematician, an expert on the art of navigation, an astronomer. But he was also the royal astrologer, the person to whom Elizabeth had turned to find an auspicious day for her coronation. And he believed that his queen, through English conquest of the New World, was the successor to the legendary King Arthur, leader of the Round Table.

Footsteps thudded against damp wood, and light flooded the dock far below him. He paid little attention until there was a sudden silence, followed by the lighter clack of a woman's shoes. No further announcement was necessary. He started for his library at once.

Dee's house brimmed with the trappings of his work, but no room so well reflected his interests as his library. Part study, part laboratory, part magician's lair, it was full not only of books but of the greatest array of scientific instruments assembled in England, possibly the world. The heavy oak door swung open and the queen sailed into the room.

"Well, Dr. Dee," Elizabeth said, taking a seat in front of a long table, breathing in the smell of musty books and dust and finding them, as she always did when she came to Dee's house, oddly comforting. "Here we are. Come to consult the wisest man of the age."

"I'm no more than the interpreter, Majesty. The wisdom lies in the planets and the stars." He sat across from her and picked up an astrological chart. "Your dominant sign here is Virgo—"

She laughed. "Of course."

"As Virgo comes into the ascendant, twelve days before the anniversary of your birth"—he lifted another chart, this one astronomical—"there will be an eclipse of the moon—the moon which governs the fortunes of all princes of the female gender." His attention was back on the astrological chart.

"Princes of the female gender," the queen said, smiling and looking across the room at Walsingham, who was idly examining the scientific instruments. He didn't appear to be listening, but she knew he was.

"I mean to say a prince who is also a woman."

"Yes, Dr. Dee. I am following you. So what does it all mean?"

"It means the rise of a great empire, Majesty. And it means convulsions, also. The fall of an empire."

"Which empire is to rise, and which is to fall?" she asked.

"That I can't say. Astrology is, as yet, more an art than a science."

"Nothing more, Dr. Dee?" Walsingham asked. "No more specific calamities that we can guard against?"

"He's asking if I'll be assassinated," Elizabeth said.

"Queens are mortal," Walsingham said.

Dee shook his head, spoke gently. "Elizabeth is mortal. The queen will never die."

"You see, Francis? This is a mystery." She raised an eyebrow at her advisor, then turned to Dee. "He has no patience with mysteries."

"What I don't know, I can't use," Walsingham said.

"And yet mysteries have power. Have you not learned that?" Dee asked.

"Francis, leave us alone for a moment." She had another question, one that required privacy, one that she was ashamed to admit felt more pressing to her heart than the issues of empires. Walsingham left and her voice lightened as she tried to sound flip, only vaguely interested. "And the private life of this prince of the female gender, Dr. Dee? What do the stars foretell there?"

"The private life?"

"Or is this too a mystery?" she asked. She wanted to say his name—the way a person does when she's in love, eager for any excuse to feel those perfect syllables on her lips. Raleigh. But she had enough control to resist.

"These are matters of state, Majesty."

Matters of state. Of course. Her private life would never be private.

"Do the stars not foretell matters of state?" she asked.

"For such a prediction, I must look in a different chart." That chart was her face, and he came close to her, studying it, murmuring half out loud, half to himself. "Wonderful . . . out of such suffering, to have forged such strength . . . You will need all your strength in days to come . . . And love . . . so much love."

So much love. He could only mean Raleigh. She was certain. There was no one else—not anymore. The doctor continued to search her face, and she held her breath, waiting for him to say more about this love, but instead he recited the words of St. Paul:

"'This corruptible must put on incorruption, and this mortal must put on immortality.'" He went to the window, back to the night sky. "No, I'm no prophet. I see no more than the shadows of ghosts."

"Shadows. I understand." Thick disappointment laced her voice, and she wondered if he offered nothing further because he saw nothing else, or because he knew that his visions would not please her. She could order him to tell her, but something kept her from doing that, a small feeling of doubt burning low in her stomach, whispering that Raleigh would not, for her, be the source of any enduring love.

Chapter 10

Bess had not returned from the docks. She'd sent a message to inform the queen that she was going to stay with her mother, whom she'd decided to visit on her way back to the palace, and Elizabeth felt mildly irritated to find that she missed the girl. It was unaccountable, really. She had plenty of other ladies at her disposal, but none had shared with her the effortless friendship like the one she had with Bess.

She'd tried to play chess with one of them, but the woman was either too dimwitted or too afraid to beat her, and the game came to a rapid yet tedious close. She'd gone to her music room, played her virginals, but no one's voice harmonized with hers so well as Bess's. She'd looked out her window in the direction of Durham House and wondered what her Water was doing. He'd not come to see her, which was a surprise. She'd expected him to storm in, demanding to know why she'd sent Bess to check up on him. But he'd kept away. Perhaps she should have gone herself.

The thought brought a smile to her face. The queen appearing, unannounced, in a shipyard? It was an appealing idea that would cause a satisfying flurry of spontaneous admiration. And when he was next at sea—when she told him he could go—he would remember her on deck, in his cabin, and she would stay nearer to his heart. Yes. She would tour his ship. Tomorrow, perhaps, if the weather was good. Or next week. Someday.

That decided, she felt somewhat better, but was still distracted. After picking up and rejecting no fewer than a dozen books, she went to her bedchamber, sending all her ladies from the room as soon as they'd washed her face and removed her gown and jewels. Alone now, she let her shift fall to the floor in a crumpled heap and she stood, naked, before a long mirror. She gazed at her reflection, lamplight dancing around her, bouncing from the mirror to the walls and back again in endless cycles.

She touched her stomach, her arms.

Her skin was not as firm as it had once been, but her muscles were strong, and her figure as fine as any. She tried to imagine growing old with a man, someone who would see the changes in her body as a visible reminder of happy years spent together, who would know the source of every scar and the location of every imperfection and adore them all. Someone who, above all, would never let her feel so very alone. If such a thing were even possible. But surely it was.

It had to be.

❧

Reston had gone to St. Paul's for inspiration, and as he sat in the middle of the cathedral's nave, anonymous in the huge building, the desire to bring glory to God consumed him. When he was finished, when England had returned to the true faith, he would come back here and restore this church's ornamentation; make it reflect, once again, divine greatness.

It was a great motivator, something he needed more than ever now. The loss of Throckmorton was a blow, not simply because it meant the loss of a reliable agent but because it meant his group had been compromised and he knew not how. Had the heretic queen's spymaster sent agents to follow Throckmorton? How had they known of his involvement? Had the man's cousin, this woman called Bess, given him up to save herself from suspicion? Worse still was another thought, that Walsingham had not simply uncovered part of their scheme but that one of his men had infiltrated their group. That one among them was not loyal.

He sank to his knees, asking God for a sign, confirmation of his cohorts' loyalty. After praying for more than an hour, he felt the glow of divine confidence wash through him, and he knew that God had not abandoned him, had not allowed his mission to be seriously threatened. Still, despite his certainty, his feeling of relief, he did what anyone in his position would.

He returned to his rooms and called each of the members of his group to him, individually, and questioned them more thoroughly than Walsingham himself could have. Before night fell, he was satisfied with his human confirmation of God's message and ready to continue his work.

But first, he would pray for Throckmorton's soul.

THE WAIT FOR THIS week's delivery seemed endless. Reston was trying to compose a letter, but his hand ached, tension seeping into every muscle, making it difficult to write. Candles lit the hidden cellar room in which he sat, their flickering glow far from bright. He leapt to his feet when the brewer walked in. "You have it?" he asked. Burton handed him a letter, which Reston read and passed to another man, hidden in the shadows, face covered by a hood. "What do you think? You're the expert on church law."

His companion shook his head as he read. "No. It won't do. This is not an order." Mary had to do more than agree to their plans. She was their true sovereign—she had to command that Elizabeth be assassinated. She had to set their scheme into motion. He was adamant on this point.

Reston nodded agreement, returned to the table, and dashed off a letter. "She and she alone must give the order," he said, passing his now-complete note to Burton. "One more journey, my friend. Then—*consummatum est!* It is finished."

Excitement pulsed through him. They were so close. He would pray now and, when he was finished, allow himself to start work on his plans for St. Paul's. Truly, there was no enjoyment more satisfying than that of bringing souls and glory to God.

THE PURSUIT OF PLEASURE was always within reach of Elizabeth's court, regardless of which royal palace they occupied. The queen often rose late—she'd never been fond of mornings—and though most of her time was spent on government matters, she was no stranger to the arts of entertainment. Her homes had tennis courts, elaborate garden mazes, spaces for command performances of the latest plays. She hunted stag and cheered enthusiastically while watching her trained mastiffs set to the bloody work of bearbaiting. But dancing was the pastime to which she continually returned, a pursuit that allowed for rare intimacy and physical satisfaction. It would always carry memories of Robert, the partner of her youth, and though thoughts of him were always laced with the bittersweet, she welcomed them.

"Jump!" The dancing master clapped as he commanded Bess, instructing her in la volta. It was full of leaping and turning and exuberant emotion, but it was the intimate embrace required by the dance that brought its wild popularity. They were in Elizabeth's atrium, a trio of musicians playing a jaunty tune as a circle of ladies watched Bess.

"When I push like this, my lady, give a jump into the air."

"Let him throw you round, Bess," the queen said. "You can trust him."

He spun the girl, her feet flying out, and lifted her into the air as the watching courtiers laughed. "And round—and round—and round—and down!" He lowered her to the ground. Her lovely face, flushed from the exercise, was bright, her eyes sparkling, lips parted in a beguiling smile. As the spinning began again, Raleigh entered the room.

"La volta, Water," Elizabeth said as he crossed to her, his focus on the dancers. "The jump. I require all my ladies to learn it. You see how fearless Bess is."

He could not take his eyes off her. Fearless. Beautiful. Sweet. Vulnerable. He remembered the feeling of Bess's skin against his, remembered the sweet taste of her tongue, and felt an odd jealousy at the fact that the queen had so much control over her. "You like your ladies to jump at your command?"

"Sometimes. Do you think that is wrong?"

"No, no. You're the queen. You are to be obeyed."

"To tell you the truth, Water, there are times when I'm tired of being always in control."

"Nonsense," he said, forcing himself to pay attention to Elizabeth when all he wanted was to drink in every detail of Bess. He had to be more careful; he could not trust himself to hide his passion.

"What?" Regal eyebrows rose.

"You don't mean a word of it. You eat and drink control."

"Do you think so?" she asked as the music stopped and the courtiers clapped. "Bess, you must try a dance with Mr. Raleigh. He's eager to show us his skill."

"No skill at all, Majesty. I don't know the steps."

"Oh, it's very simple." The queen stood, crossed the room to Bess and held her by the waist to demonstrate. "You stand like this, with your hands firmly clasped here—and when she jumps, on the eighth step, you swing her round—once, twice, three times—and you're back to the beginning. What could be simpler?"

"Your Majesty knows the dance better than I," the dancing master said, bowing low.

"So come, Mr. Raleigh. Take your position." Elizabeth urged him forward. "I am to be obeyed."

"As Your Majesty wishes," Raleigh replied with a flourish, taking his place next to Bess, tempering his feelings, trying not to look too eager, hoping she would understand.

"Hold her tight. I don't want her dropped," Elizabeth said, then commanded the musicians. "Play!"

The dance began again, and they started to move. Raleigh's touch was too tentative at first, and her jump was awkward, but then their eyes met, and it was as if the world around them vanished. Now they moved together flawlessly, Bess jumping, Raleigh swinging her round and round.

"I wish we were alone," he whispered as he picked her up to swing her.

"As do I," she replied, smiling.

"We have to be very careful, Bess." But try though they might, they could not hide their intensity, their intimacy, their longing. It was obvious to anyone paying half attention.

ELIZABETH STUDIED THE COUPLE on the floor, nodding to the beat. She felt Walsingham come to her side.

"Majesty, if you would like I will—"

"Leave her alone, Walsingham. I want both of them left alone." She was not so confident as her voice suggested, but she liked seeing the passion in Raleigh's eyes, and she could see the pleasure Bess drew from it.

Her emotions were a tumble of confusion. It would be dangerous to try to keep them apart when their attraction was so apparent. Better to let them enjoy each other, to bring them together enough that they would not have to seek each other out privately. So long as she was careful that they could never meet outside of her presence, there was no danger that he would entirely transfer his affections to the girl. Besides, this was what she'd warned Bess of: men and their desires. They meant so very little, were utterly indiscriminate. Any of her ladies might incite in him the same response. There was no point in denying him his flirtation.

She wanted him all to herself but knew that she could not have that unless she gave him the same in return. Raleigh spun Bess around again, and the girl laughed with such perfect delight that, for an instant, Elizabeth wanted nothing more than to laugh like that herself, even if it meant giving everything to one man.

Bess had a terrible time falling asleep that night, and when she did, her dreams would not allow for peaceful slumber. She saw Raleigh, too far away, and knew she'd betrayed him, though not how or why. She was trapped just beyond consciousness, fitful, restless, at last waking up with a start, stifling a scream with her hand as she sat up in her bed. Across the room, Walsingham sat in a stiff-backed chair, watching her, silent, his presence more frightening than her dream, bringing instantly to mind hideous thoughts of her cousin's execution.

"Please! I'm innocent," she said. "I've always been a loyal servant of the queen. My cousin was nothing to me. I'd never betray the queen, never—"

"But you have, my dear." His voice was preternaturally calm. "And you do. We both know that."

She knew at once that he meant her affair with Raleigh, and it terrified her. Terrified her that Walsingham might harm her lover, keep her from ever seeing him—touching him—again. The illicit nature of their relationship made it full of peril; they both knew it, had talked about it long into the night until red light streaked the sky. But neither of them was able to will away the consuming feelings drawing them together.

Now that Walsingham was here, however, she started to question her decisions and could bring herself neither to look at nor to speak to the man.

His sharp voice shattered the silence. "Keep me informed, and all will be well," he said, standing. "I don't like surprises."

"I— I—" She fumbled to reply, but he was already gone. His footsteps were silent, but she heard a soft click as he closed the door behind him. It felt as if her bones had dissolved. She collapsed in a heap on her bed, relieved, scared, wanting nothing but Raleigh's arms around her again. First she couldn't breathe, then she couldn't stop crying.

She should force herself to stop loving him, should refuse to see him again, and thank God that they'd gone this far without being caught or arrested. But these sentiments she let into her head only because she knew they were what she was supposed to think—what was strictly right, moral—and she forced them from her mind almost before they were fully formed. No matter the risk, she could not keep away from him. To pretend anything else was no better than a lie.

She dried her eyes with her linen sheet and sat up tall, feeling strong again. She waited an hour before she left her room and, in the cloak of darkness, slipped away to Durham House. Raleigh was the only person on earth who could understand her emotions.

To ANY OBSERVER, MARY Stuart's piety would have appeared moving, so focused was she on her prayer, head bent low in the modest chapel at Chartley Hall. But the Bible that hid her face was not providing inspiration. Behind it, she was writing a letter, out of the sight of her jailers. It was a frequent occurrence, though not all her correspondence merited such secrecy. She thrilled at the game of it, the sensations it caused, the up-and-down emotions that reminded her of falling in love.

Today, though, her confidence was tempered. This note was more important than any she'd written in her life, and she had to be certain she phrased everything in a precise manner. She trusted her friends but was too smart to be careless. She bent her head low, almost resting it on the table as she wrote, and this drew the attention of her warden. Careful not to move too quickly, she closed the paper into the book when Paulet stepped toward her, three men following behind him.

"Am I a danger to England even when I pray?" she asked.

"As always, ma'am, my concern is for your safety."

Paulet's voice was kind, but Mary noticed a difference in his smile. She looked at him with a cool stare. "I pray for my cousin Elizabeth. Do you think she prays for me?"

"I've no doubt of it," Paulet replied. "She is a holy woman."

"Is she?" Mary threw back her head and laughed. "Yet she holds a sovereign ruler prisoner. I would not be so ungenerous."

"What would you have her do?"

"Release me. So that I might find love again." She fought back a sigh, displeased that he'd not shown any reaction to this statement. "I suppose that's a hopeless cause."

"I'm sure you'll find consolation in the Bible."

The men retreated but didn't leave her alone, hovering near the door, taking turns walking past her at irregular intervals. The rest of her letter would have to wait.

❧

Mary's letter came much later than Reston had expected, late enough that he'd begun to worry, but at last it had arrived. In their hidden room in London, Babington and Ramsay sat, watching, faces tense with anxiety, as he read aloud. During all the months they'd spent holed up in the squalid place, they'd done nothing to improve its conditions. Water seeped through cracks between the rough rocks that formed the walls, and the smell of mildew had long since permeated their clothes, books, every porous thing. They shared the space with any number of sordid little creatures, most of whom scurried away at the slightest hint of light. But the conspirators hadn't many candles, and more often than not, their work was accompanied by the sound of gnawing teeth and the click of tiny feet against stone.

"If our forces are in readiness, both within and without the realm, then your Queen commands you to set the gentlemen to work." He smiled, eyes unholy in their brightness. "I think we have it." He handed the letter to a figure who stepped out of the shadows, wanting him to see the words for himself.

"Yes," William Walsingham said, pulling down his hood and revealing his face. "We have it now."

Reston turned to his men. "At last. Gentlemen, to work." His heart soared, and he murmured a joyful prayer, eager to begin. With each step now, he was moving closer to heaven.

Chapter 11

"I speak more languages than you," Elizabeth said, leaning against the back of the stone bench and stretching her legs, breathing in the good scent of lavender. She and Raleigh had spent the morning wandering through her gardens, and she was quite certain they'd walked no fewer than five miles.

"More, perhaps, but are they useful? I've little danger of encountering natives fluent in Latin on my travels."

"Spanish might be helpful."

"True," he said, picking up her hand. "I could make you my translator."

"What would my official title be?" she asked.

"I'm not sure, but you'd be badly paid and treated in a most appalling manner."

She laughed. "So long as you don't make me clean the deck."

"Swab. We swab the deck." He leaned close, his voice intimate, teasing. "You are not fluent in the language of sailors."

"You could teach me," she said. "I'm a good pupil."

"I doubt that very much. You'd never be able to stand someone telling you what to do."

"I might if he had the right manner while doing it."

"My manner is always right."

"Is it?" she asked. "I wonder."

"I could show you."

"That would be dangerous," she said, loving the way every inch of her skin came alive when he flirted with her.

"I might be worth the risk," he said.

RALEIGH DID NOT STAY seated after Elizabeth left him in the garden. As usual, Walsingham had pulled her away to attend to pressing business, confirming again that he would never have all of her. He kicked at the dirt on the path in front of him, making his shoes dusty. He'd told her he might be worth the risk, and the words were so close to ones he'd said to Bess. Love was not supposed to bring with it this sort of agony. How had he managed to fall simultaneously in love with two unattainable women?

He was leading them both on, selfishly taking what he could from each. But he sought only that which was given freely, and at least Bess knew how divided his affections were. And Elizabeth . . . it was unlikely he could ever hide something from her. He knew not what to do except continue through these murky waters, hoping that eventually a solution would emerge and wash away the guilt that for now was his constant companion.

❧

Francis Walsingham was buried in work, holed up in his study at his house on Seething Lane, reading a letter from Thomas Phelippes, more pleased than ever with his decision to found a school of cryptography in London, smug at his continuing success as he was every time he saw Phelippes's work.

Today's delivery from his cipher secretary was the culmination of all their work. Mary had at last given specific instructions to her allies, showing great concern for the precise timing of her release and Elizabeth's assassination. In the margin, Phelippes had added a symbol: Π. The gallows. Mary could no longer escape her guilt. The postscript had not even been necessary.

And all this should have brought Walsingham joy. Or, if not joy, certainly contentedness, a feeling of accomplishment, satisfaction. But his pleasure was tainted. This was a dirty business, and it had stained his soul. Ferreting out secrets could lead to abysmal disappointment. He read Mary's letter again, then tossed it aside, picking up a pen and fiddling with it as he considered the queen's likely response to this new proof of her cousin's treachery.

There was one final piece still missing. He knew the conspirators were going to act—that Elizabeth was in grave danger—but he knew not when they would strike. He'd already ordered protective measures. More soldiers were on their way to Whitehall, and the number of soldiers guarding the queen herself had doubled. He hoped it would be enough.

A knock sounded on his door. "Enter," he said but did not look up from his papers.

"It's me. William."

Still he did not look up. "Where have you been?" Walsingham said. "We haven't seen you for days."

"I met up with some old friends." William stepped forward, one smooth, well-groomed hand reaching for the back of a chair, the other concealed under his cloak.

"From Paris, no doubt."

"Yes."

"And now you've come back." He looked up at last. "Do you know, I can still remember the day you were born?" The smile on Walsingham's lips was at odds with the sadness in his eyes. "I was eleven years old. And you, this helpless bundle. I looked at you in your crib, with your little wrinkled face, and I loved you from the first. I vowed then to look after you. But I've failed you, haven't I? Forgive me if I haven't loved you enough."

The brothers looked at each other for a long moment, a matched recognition reflecting between their eyes. With a clatter, something fell from William's hand. His face had gone gray.

"Did you really think I didn't know?" Walsingham looked at the dagger on the floor, then rapped twice on his desk, bringing two of his agents into the room. "Was it for money? At least tell me you got a good price."

William shook his head. The inconspicuous-looking men wrenched his arms behind him, moving with a fluidity that told how often they restrained prisoners.

"What then? What would you murder your own brother for?" No trace of anger mixed with Walsingham's sadness.

"Eternal life."

"Eternal life," Walsingham repeated. Pain distorted his features, his eyes closed, mouth twisted, cheeks sunken. "The bribe no man can refuse."

Whose God would be happy tonight?

From the instant morning had dawned, it had been as if Whitehall had been warmed by a divine smile. Sunshine danced between clouds and bounced off the jewels covering the courtiers' bright clothing, an ocean of reds, purples, and blues. Supplicants swarmed to line the path from the Presence Chamber to the Chapel Royal, eager as always to catch a glimpse of the queen in the midst of her magnificent procession.

Babington and Ramsay were immune to the charms of the scene. They didn't notice any beauty, only the stench of too many bodies too close together in the summer heat.

Babington's stomach burned as he watched his new partner and remembered Savage's fate, but he pushed away the feelings of guilt. He had done what was necessary. Ramsay was more stable than Savage had ever been, more dependable. There was no doubt their mission would succeed.

Babington could hear his blood moving through his ears and his heart pounded, but he steadied his nerves and flashed a discreet hand signal to Ramsay, who returned it with the slightest nod. At once, they forced their way swiftly to the front of the crowd, just as Elizabeth disappeared from view into the dark safety of the church.

"The queen is at her prayers!" a servant in livery announced as the doors began to shut.

"Now!" Babington cried, and Ramsay hurled himself forward, shouting.

"God for Mary! England's true queen!"

There were more guards than he'd seen before, and they ran to seize Ramsay, opening a momentary space in the crush of confusion, a space through which Babington sprinted, bursting through the closing doors and into the chapel. In the dim light, he saw a line of ladies kneeling, masking the figure in front of the altar.

He pulled out his pistol. "Elizabeth!"

She turned around, tall, exuding a composed confidence, rising to confront the assassin's gun, no sign of fear on her proud face. Babington stared, hypnotized for an instant, then pulled the trigger.

❧

Elizabeth did not move, not even at the sound of the shot, holding herself steady as relief rushed through her when she realized she felt no pain, had not been wounded. She watched her assailant cry out in anguish and crumple to the ground, wounded but not dead. A bullet had flown but not from his gun, and a strong smell of gunpowder filled the chapel.

Never before had she felt more regal, untouchable, magnificent. Strength filled her veins till they felt as if they would burst. No one else in the chapel had remained standing. First, they'd dropped to the ground, afraid of the gun. Now they stayed down, supplicants abasing themselves before their glorious leader.

God had protected His queen.

❧

"Stories of your courage have entirely overshadowed all other gossip in court," Raleigh said. Elizabeth had perfectly maintained her composure after the attack, shown no weakness. She'd insisted on finishing her prayers as if nothing had happened and had processed back to the palace holding her head high. But when she'd disappeared into the safe darkness of her bedchamber, she'd broken down, scared and overwhelmed. Raleigh had come to her even before she'd sent for him.

"I'm not so brave, Water."

"I think you are."

"Not anymore," she said, her voice rough.

"If you did not give in to private moments of terror after such an occurrence, you would not be human."

"Should a queen dare to be human?" she asked. Tears were starting again, and she turned so he would not see them.

"Not even a queen has a choice in the matter. You are human, Elizabeth."

He'd not called her by her name before, and the sound of his voice saying it was like the song of angels. "Thank you for coming to me. Thank you for not making me ask for you."

He took her hands. "I would like nothing more than to ensure you never need ask for another thing."

"Would that it were even possible."

He smiled. "You are the queen. You can make anything possible."

And just then, she almost believed him.

Chapter 12

Mary was pacing impatiently, Geddon trailing behind her, the walls of her room pressing with unbearable force on her soul. She'd memorized every thread of every tapestry on the walls and counted the squares on the gleaming parquet floor, and still the clock's hand made small progress. It was as if time had stopped passing. She could not focus her thoughts, could not calm her nerves, could not bear to wait another moment.

Fantasy had grown exhausting. She had envisioned her freedom, pondered being made a queen again, wondered what the English throne would feel like—these thoughts had consumed her for weeks, and she could no longer stand the agony of waiting. She moved her lips, praying silently, hands on her rosary, fingering first the golden crucifix, then the beads, and then—finally—the sound of bells floated in through the window, carrying with it a flood of joy. She heard footsteps and pulled herself up straight, regal, serene. Sir Amyas hurried through the open door toward her.

"You bring news?" she asked. Her ladies had come to her side, faces shining with hope.

"The queen has been attacked—"

Her heart was pounding violently as she opened her eyes wide. She had to look surprised. "Elizabeth? Not my cousin? No!"

"The assassin seized—"

It was unbearable. "Yes?"

"The queen unharmed—"

"Unharmed?" There was an unmistakable edge in Mary's voice, anger, disbelief, and at last, genuine surprise.

"And you, ma'am," Paulet said with a smile, "are under arrest."

"Me? What has any of this to do with me?" she asked, doing her best to lure him with her soft voice and suggestive eyes while fear filled every cell of her body.

Paulet made a sign and Burton, the brewer, came into the room. Mary gasped when she saw him. Tears stung in her eyes, but she held them back.

"That's the trouble with intrigue, isn't it?" Paulet asked. "With so many secrets, you can never quite tell who's on whose side, until the game ends." He pulled from his pocket the hollow bung used to hide her letters in the beer caskets and admired it. "My own invention. Theatrical but effective. My master has every letter you've written."

"Your master?" Her voice was rapidly losing confidence.

"Walsingham."

Now she let herself weep. "Traitors. I'm surrounded by traitors. Who am I to trust?" Geddon stood below her, wagging his tail earnestly. "Only my little one." Crying bitterly, she picked him up, held him to her face, and wondered how long she would have to prepare for the end.

WATER SPLASHED WALSINGHAM'S SHOES as he climbed out of the boat and stepped onto the cool stone of the walk. The yeoman warder admitted him to the Tower without a word, giving him a sharp, respectful nod as he passed through Traitor's Gate. He crossed Tower Green, untroubled by shadows and stories of ghosts—though as always, he could not help but glance at the spot where Elizabeth's mother had been executed—a grim reminder of how far even a queen could fall.

He walked on, then stopped at a half-timbered building between Beauchamp Tower and the Queen's House to speak with the gentleman gaoler who supervised the prisoners and their guards. They drank dark, bitter beer as they discussed state business, Walsingham in no rush to continue on his way. As the moon rose high in the dark sky, he could delay no longer. He accepted a lamp from the gaoler and descended into the bowels of the Tower.

All the conspirators, save Mary, were now in the Tower. Mary, they had decided, would be kept separate from the men who had worked on her behalf. Walsingham had succeeded in protecting his queen, but he moved through the dank passage with no joy, instead bowed down by a sense of failure. He held up the lamp to look through cell bars at the prisoner inside.

"Ready to die, I see, Jesuit," he said.

No fear showed on Reston's face. He was calm, arrogant. "I have done what I was sent to do."

"Why was the gun not loaded?" Walsingham asked, but received no reply. Reston had fallen to his knees and was praying. He stood, watching the priest for a moment longer, then moved the lamp and saw the pale faces of Babington and Ramsay. He studied them but said nothing, steeling himself for what he would find in the next cell. The man inside it lay in chains, huddled on the floor. As the light Walsingham carried illuminated the space, William raised his head.

Walsingham tasted bile. "What was the Jesuit sent to do?" he asked.

"To kill the queen. You know it. You know everything," his brother answered.

"Not quite everything."

"I've told you all I know. Go ahead and kill me. Take what's left of me. I don't care anymore. All my life you've had everything and I've had nothing. So finish it. There's a better world waiting for me. We'll all be judged in the end, brother. Even you."

"You're no martyr," Walsingham said, unmoved by this show of pride. "You weren't even much of a murderer. Go back to France. Never let me hear of you again." He turned his back to the man on the floor, not wanting him to see the hurt of a betrayal almost too much to bear painted over his face. He went back up the passage, looking no more at the prisoners, not pausing even when Reston called out to him in a soft voice almost like a song:

"Send me home."

THE INFANTA PAID SCANT attention to the booming voices of the men around her as she played in the throne room at the Escorial Palace. She'd slid off her small throne onto the polished marble floor, liking the way her heavy skirts billowed around her when she plopped down, dolls in her hands. She pushed against the richly embroidered fabric, smoothing it against her stiff whalebone farthingale, then lined up her dolls. The tallest of them, the one that looked like the queen of England, was her favorite. They told her the queen was called Elizabeth and that her hair blazed like fire, a red the child thought better suited to a doll than a real woman. Queens should have dark hair, like hers.

Her father, Philip, was behind her, talking to Don Guerau de Spes, a man the infanta didn't much like. His breath was sour and he stood too close when he talked to her. But her father seemed to like him. He squinted his eyes, and his ringed fingers rested still on the arm of his golden throne, all signs that he was listening intently. They were talking about England, something about it being saved. She made her Elizabeth doll walk over to another and knock it to the floor.

"They have letters in Mary Stuart's own hand," Don Guerau was saying. "All England cries out for her death."

The girl perked at the sound of the name. Mary. She was a queen, too. Now she not only disliked Don Guerau, she knew he was foolish. A queen could not be killed. She looked toward her father, expecting him to say just that, but he only reached down, stroked her hair, and asked her a simple question:

"My dearest, how would you like to be Queen of England?"

Chapter 13

"Read me another," Bess said, stretching out on the enormous bed, pulling the sheet up to her chin, burying her head in a stack of downy pillows.

"You're insatiable," Raleigh said.

"Yes. For your poems."

"Nothing else?"

"That remains to be seen," she said. "Read!"

"Passion are liken'd best to floods and streams: / The shallow murmur, but the deep are dumb; / So, when affection yields discourse, it seems / The bottom is but shallow whence they come. / They that are rich in words, in words discover / That they are poor in that which makes a lover."

"You, my dear, are rich both in words and those things that make a lover." She rolled closer to him and put her head on his chest. "Your poem is a lie. Write me a better one."

"I will, but not this afternoon, when there are so many better occupations before me."

"I must be back at the palace before dark."

"We've time enough." He kissed her. "And you wouldn't dare rush me."

Elizabeth let the chamber grow dark around her, refused to admit the maid who wanted to light the lamps. Someone had brought a tray of food that sat, untouched, congealing, on a table. Outside in the atrium, courtiers hovered, taking turns listening at the door, hearing only silence. Not even the sound of pacing steps to break the monotony. Bess pushed through them and burst into the room.

"I told them not to let anyone but you come in," Elizabeth said, watching as Bess closed the door, sinking her again into darkness. "Sit with me." The queen was sitting in a tall-backed wainscot chair, elaborately carved from oak, lacking anything that might offer comfort, no pad on its narrow seat. Her father had used it in his youth, and she'd always felt unaccountably sentimental about it. Bess crossed the room slowly as her eyes adjusted to the dim light and sat on the floor at Elizabeth's feet.

"They say she's taller than me," Elizabeth said. "Her hair is auburn in color. Her eyes are blue. Some say she's beautiful. I've seen her portrait, and she does seem to me to be beautiful. But portraits lie. I've never seen her in my life."

"Nor have I, Majesty."

Elizabeth took Bess's hand, thinking about all the times Walsingham had come to her with evidence against

Mary. He wanted the fallen queen brought to trial after Throckmorton's scheme unraveled; Elizabeth had refused. The Privy Council had passed, in 1584, a Bond of Association, which Parliament voted into law the following year. Any person with claims to the throne of England who knew about a plot against the queen would lose his—or her—place in the line of succession and be put to death, the former punishment rather underwhelming, given the latter. The law had slightly modified the bond presented by the Privy Council: their version insisted that the claimant should be put to death even if he had no knowledge of plans to overthrow the current monarch. Standing to benefit from such treachery would have been enough to prove guilt. But Mary, now, was implicated much further.

"They say she plotted to kill you."

"Yes, it's true. I've read her letters."

"They say she must die."

"They say—they say." Elizabeth rose from her chair, the backs of her legs pushing it against the wall, and stalked toward the window. "She's a queen, Bess. Or was, for a time. My mother was a queen. For a time. I was not even three years old when—when her life was cut short." Elizabeth closed her eyes, fighting the beginnings of a headache. Her memories of Anne Boleyn came from other people's stories; she didn't even have hazy visions of her own. They told her she'd been a passionate woman, vivacious, with a wit that had captivated the king. And that she'd loved her little daughter with all her soul, visiting the baby at Hatfield House, where Elizabeth had been sent soon after her birth.

Elizabeth had not inherited her mother's dark eyes, nearly black, that were said to have mesmerized her father. But Anne had been unfaithful to the king and was found guilty of adultery and treason and executed on Tower Green. She'd asked for a French executioner, whose sharp sword would be more likely to take only one swift stroke to sever her head, an end far preferable to multiple clumsy blows of a heavy axe.

There were other rumors, though. Rumors that the charges against Queen Anne were lies. That she'd never betrayed Henry. That her inability to produce a son led to her downfall. That her beautiful daughter, Elizabeth, had not been enough to satisfy the king.

"Oh, I dread this act. I dread it with all my soul." Elizabeth had begun to sway. Bess steadied her. "Thank you, Bess. I could not do without your friendship." The girl blushed and called for a servant to bring lavender tea, but the queen would not drink it, succumbing instead to the painful misery growing in her head.

"Again you come to me," Elizabeth said, offering Raleigh her hand as he bowed in front of her.

"I knew you would be troubled. But you cannot doubt that she must be brought to trial," he said.

"I don't fear the trial, only the verdict."

"The law must be obeyed."

"Queens are not subject to ordinary laws."

"Think on it no more," he said. "There's nothing more to be done until judgment is passed, and you must find something else to occupy your mind lest you drive yourself mad."

"So, amuse me, Water, make yourself endlessly distracting."

"Call for your musicians. I want to dance with you."

She obeyed him and found herself surprisingly thrilled at this small act of submission. They danced until they were both so tired they could hardly draw breath, until the musicians looked as if they would collapse from exhaustion and the courtiers who watched knew without doubt that the queen had fallen in love.

Chapter 14

Fotheringay Castle stood bleak and unwelcoming on the fens some seventy miles from London, an imposing gathering place for the nobles of the realm who'd come to watch the trial of Mary Stuart. Elizabeth had appointed commissioners—thirty-six of them—to hear the case and determine a verdict. They came from the most noble families in her realm, were men she trusted above all others. No one else could be in charge of something so grave.

Mary had managed to delay the commission by refusing to participate. She was a queen, a sovereign, not subject to the laws of England, and insisted the trial was illegal. But in the end, Sir Christopher Hatton had persuaded her to let it continue. He would allow her complaint to be formally recorded—but without a trial, she would never have the opportunity to prove her innocence.

The night before the proceedings were to begin, she

found a letter from her cousin tucked casually next to a plate on her dinner tray. She picked it up, fingered the paper, noted that Elizabeth's italics were as perfectly elegant as ever, but hesitated to open it. After two bites of bread and a flavorless spoonful of some thin soup of ambiguous origin, she broke the seal.

> *You have in various ways and manners attempted to take my life and to bring my kingdom to destruction by bloodshed. I have never proceeded so harshly against you, but have, on the contrary, protected and maintained you like myself. These treasons will be proved to you and all made manifest. Yet it is my will that you answer the nobles and peers of the kingdom as if I were myself present. I therefore require, charge, and command that you make answer, for I have been well informed of your arrogance.*
>
> *Act plainly, without reserve, and you will sooner be able to obtain favor of me.*
>
> *Elizabeth*

Her cousin's words incensed her. She pushed her food away from her, knocking over a heavy goblet, wine leaving a dark stain on the table. She started to pace. "I have not threatened her," she said, clutching Geddon to her chest with one hand while she shook the paper at her ladies with the other. "I have plotted desperately to secure my own safety—to escape from these prisons to which I've been confined. I have ordered men to assist me. But I have not planned to kill a queen."

She pulled out a stack of papers she'd carried with her from Chartley House and motioned for Annette to sit with her. She had the sharpest mind of any of Mary's ladies and was the best suited to help her put the finishing touches on her defense.

"Here," she said, thrusting the pages at Annette. "Read these while I continue writing." She had started work on her statement the day Paulet had told her of the charges against her and continued to polish her words every day since they had brought her to Fotheringay.

"They cannot find you guilty," Annette said when she reached the end of the first page.

"I hope you're right," Mary said. "After twenty years as a prisoner, I fear I grew complacent. I've done everything I could to organize an escape."

"And you were always thwarted," Annette said.

"Yes, but even when plots were discovered, I was never implicated. It gave me a dangerous sense of security."

"Do you know what they claim as evidence against you?"

"Not precisely. My letters, I assume." She tried to remember exactly what she'd written in that last missive. They had asked her to give them orders, to issue the command, and she'd done that—but she'd phrased her words with great care, stopping short of directly telling them to assassinate Elizabeth. Of course, it was evident that the queen's death was part of the plan, but how could she be held accountable for that? She was not the author of the scheme.

"So, these Englishmen," Annette said. "They can be sent to their deaths for being party to a threat to the queen?"

"Yes."

"But you are not English."

"Precisely. Perhaps if I am able to distance myself from the conspirators, that will be enough. I am not responsible for their plans."

Annette finished with the papers and an ugly laugh flew from her throat. "These people are so pathetic. You, madam, have the strongest legal claim as Elizabeth's heir. Would they send to death the successor to their throne, when their own queen is a dried-up spinster? Who would they have rule when she is gone?"

"My son, of course." Mary sighed, thinking of the boy—James, King of Scotland. Not a boy, not any longer.

"Why did the English queen never marry?" Annette asked.

"I don't know. But she will make herself ridiculous as she ages. It's all fun to collect men like trinkets when you're young and beautiful, but it won't last." Mary relished the thought of her cousin, old and alone and pathetic, the men who claim to adore her laughing behind her back. But if she wanted to be alive to see it, she needed to finish her defense.

Fog twisted through the fens the next morning, snaking around bare tree limbs and settling on dropped leaves rotting in heaps on the damp ground. Mary leaned against the window, fingering the lead cames between the diamond-shaped panes of glass, barely feeling the hard coldness of the surface. Cold did not bother her; it helped focus her mind. A sharp rap on the door announced the servants bringing her breakfast. She was not hungry but ate every morsel, pronouncing it all delicious, wanting to project nothing but contented confidence.

As soon as she'd finished eating, she was escorted downstairs. Close to a dozen gentlemen were seated around a long table in the center of the room. Benches lined the two walls parallel to the table. Sir Thomas Bromley, Lord Chancellor, sat in the first one, the rest filled with earls of the realm and other nobles. Perpendicular to the table on one side was a single long bench with a high back: here sat Sir Christopher Hatton and Sir Francis Walsingham. Of the other four men with them, she recognized only one: Sir Amyas Paulet. Against the wall near the door and opposite the other end of the table, stood a single, magnificent chair. A throne, intended for the queen, who, Mary had been told, would not appear.

She composed herself, smoothing the soft fabric of her black gown, and stood at her full height, taller than the men who brought her to face her accusers. They led her to a chair not far from Elizabeth's empty one, across from the

Lord Chancellor. She did not sit, preferring to stand while she spoke.

"So many councilors here, but none for me," she said, a charming smile on her face. Her clear voice filled the cavernous hall, the sweetness of her syllables bouncing off the hard stone walls.

"My father was a king, and I am cousin to the queen of England. I came to this country seeking protection from my enemies and the rebels in Scotland who forced me from my throne. Your good queen promised me help, yet instead of receiving it, I was taken captive.

"I cannot recognize the laws of your country because I am a queen myself. Submitting to your justice would weaken not only my own position but that of every other sovereign ruler in the world. And yet here I stand, alone, with no one to speak on my behalf. Everything I own has been taken from me, including my papers. Papers that would have helped in my defense.

"I will make no attempt to deny that I desperately want my freedom, and that I have done all I can to secure it. Is that not understandable? Would any of you gentlemen, finding yourself in similar circumstances, act in any other way? Would you not resist? Defend yourself?

"I have tried, with the help of loyal friends, to escape my bonds. But in doing so, I have wished no harm to your own Queen Elizabeth, nor have I encouraged others in planning such a scheme. But I am a queen with a claim to the throne of

England. I do not share your faith, and there are, among you, subjects who prefer me to my cousin. I cannot be held responsible for the criminal acts and sedition of such people.

"It is my faith—the faith into which I was born—for which you judge me, and I cannot stop that. You will do as you wish. And if the worst is to come, my motto will see me through: In my end is my beginning."

She'd spoken beautifully. She knew that. But when the commissioners would not let her hear the witnesses against her, nor show her the letters they claimed as evidence—letters they insisted were written in her hand—her heart sank. Her intentions, her simple desire for freedom, would not matter to the men sitting in judgment of her; she had no doubt what their verdict would be. At the end of the second day of the trial, she told them she forgave them for what she knew was inevitable.

The verdict should have come at once, but Elizabeth ordered her commissioners back to London, where all the evidence gathered by Walsingham and his cohorts was studied in the Star Chamber, a court made up primarily of the queen's Privy Councilors, and full of the same men who'd already heard Mary's case. More testimony was given, and the Scottish queen's own secretaries did not pause in their condemnation of their sovereign. Ten days later, the decision was announced at Westminster: Mary Stuart was "not only accessory and privy to the conspiracy but also an imaginer and compasser of Her Majesty's destruction."

Parliament met not long afterward and proclaimed the verdict, but Elizabeth delayed the public reading of her proclamation of the sentence for more than a month. That Mary would be put to death was obvious, and the document need not state it directly. No one doubted the execution would come quickly—all of the country was clamoring for it. But Mary would not yet be put out of her misery.

The light in Elizabeth's library was dim, not bright enough to read by, but she did not care and made no move to light more lamps. She had come here for solace and sat in silence, pressing her hands flat together, feeling the pulse of her blood in them, then pulling them apart, over and over. She ought not be so conflicted; Walsingham had shown her all the evidence. Mary's guilt was undeniable. But no one other than herself—and Mary, she supposed—appreciated the difficulties of finding a queen culpable of a capital offense. Once again, she felt her isolation, lonely even when people surrounded her. Only another queen would understand how empty adoration could be.

Walsingham came through the open door and bowed low before sitting in a chair across from her. "Majesty?"

"Is there any truth to the rumors that this all has been an elaborate conspiracy against her? Did you plan this, Moor?"

Walsingham met her eyes, his face full of confidence. "You know of my involvement. I merely provided her the means of communication. She decided to use them the way she did."

"Had she any choice?" Elizabeth dropped her hands into her lap. "What would I have done if I found myself imprisoned?"

"You were a prisoner, Majesty."

"I wanted my sister off the throne."

"But you did not actively solicit her assassination."

"No. I did not."

"Have you signed the warrant?" he asked.

"I have not yet decided if I will."

"Majesty—"

She rose to her feet. "Do not even consider, Moor, telling me what to do. I am the queen and I shall decide my cousin's fate."

"The verdict has been proclaimed in public."

"I am perfectly aware of that. Why must I be so rushed?"

"It's been more than a month, Majesty."

"Do not pressure me," she said, rubbing her temples. "You think it is all so simple, don't you? That none of this matters beyond the ordinary rules of English law? Do you not see the precedent I am setting? That I put myself in danger by ordering her death?"

"You put yourself in danger, Majesty, by letting her live. Until she is dead, there's always the possibility of a plot to free her. Every day she remains alive gives hope to the Catholics. Do not play renegade with your own safety."

She sent him away with a wave of her hand. When the door had snapped shut behind him, she closed her eyes and focused on the sadness and confusion and anger that coursed through her. Her throat burned hot and she could feel sweat forcing its way through her makeup. She wiped her brow, then looked at her hand, upon which there was now a thick line of white lead. With a finger, she began to trace circles in the heavy lead, taking slim comfort in the repetitive motion.

Walsingham could wait. The Privy Council could wait. Time was a commodity they could not take from her, and she would sign nothing before she was ready. But Mary was waiting, too. Waiting, as Elizabeth had so many years ago in the Tower, wondering if the next time the door opened, she'd be taken to her death. It was unconscionable to do this to another human being, to another sovereign queen. She pushed back from the table, knocking over her chair as she stood, her legs shaking. Queens ought not to be so very mortal.

Chapter 15

Winter had swallowed autumn, and still Elizabeth resisted signing Mary Stuart's death warrant. Its ever-present status in her mind had led to a consuming anxiety: she was on edge, frazzled, angry. Her courtiers had started tiptoeing around her, being more obsequious than usual, and their fawning, which she ordinarily welcomed—required—had become irritating. It had been all she could do that morning not to throw a shoe at young Robert Devereux, the Earl of Essex. He was a handsome enough man, but at the moment, she had no stomach for flirting.

Even Raleigh could no longer distract her from her agitated state. The frustration on his face, in his eyes, disappointed her more than anything, though she knew she was being hard on him. She could not keep him in court forever, but she was not yet ready to let him disappear to his infinite oceans, especially now, when the problem of Mary tormented her night and day.

Parliament was clamoring for her to act, had asked her to "take away this most wicked and filthy woman." Similar things had undoubtedly been said by an earlier Parliament about her own mother. Ugly words to describe a sovereign queen.

"Your Majesty," Walsingham began, his exhaustion dark in the circles around his eyes. It was late, but she had not let him leave the Privy Chamber. "You have no choice."

"Don't tell me I have no choice! I do as I please."

"Majesty," Walsingham said. "This is no time for mercy—"

"Don't preach at me, old man." She was tired of being told what to do and was beginning to resent—violently—his persistence on this matter. She could stand it no longer. "Look at you. You can hardly stand. Go home to your wife. Go home to your bed."

"The law must have its way." He spoke calmly, but she did not reply in kind.

"The law is for common men, not for princes."

He looked at her for a long moment before he spoke, a fatherly softness in his voice. "Two rivals for a throne, one must die."

"Francis," she said, her tone more gentle as she tried to be reasonable, regal. "I owe you my life. But not my soul."

"THANK GOD YOU'VE COME," Bess said, rushing toward Raleigh as soon as he stepped into the atrium of Elizabeth's private quarters. "I've never seen her so distressed. She's been alone in her rooms since morning. She'll see no one."

"Has she asked for me?" Concern was etched in the lines on his face, but he could not help smiling at Bess. It was so hard to see her in public like this, when they were forced to ignore their feelings, to pretend their souls did not reach for each other every time their eyes met.

And there was his guilt. The guilt that came from letting the queen love him without knowing that his heart was so divided, that he'd given so much of himself to Bess. He hated to consider what she would do to Bess if she learned of their affair, hated to think of the hurt and heartbreak it would cause to all three of them. He loved both of them, these two extraordinary women, each so different. How could he step away from either?

"No. But she needs you. I know she does," she said. He took her hand in his, discreetly, needing her to know all he felt and could not say.

"Go to her." She gave him a half-smile, her lips closed, and it was enough to tell him that she understood him more perfectly than he could have hoped. He kissed her hand and left her.

The queen was sequestered in her study, sitting alone, her back to him as he entered the room. He pulled the door shut behind him, hesitated for a moment before going toward her. "My queen," he said, his Devonshire accent soft.

"My friend." She did not turn to face him. "Have you too come to tell me I must do this thing that I dread to do?"

"No. You don't need me to instruct you in your duty."

"Is it my duty? I can't do it. Since when was I so tender-hearted?"

"Since when were you so afraid?"

Now she looked at him. "Yes, I am afraid." She spoke slowly. "But what is it I fear?"

He stood, silent, considering the woman before him for a long moment, then replied. "That your soul will be touched. Royalty is close to immortality. Kill a queen, and queens are mortal."

"I spent two months in the Tower. I know what it is to be a prisoner, to fear for your life. Every day I wondered if they would come for me, take me to the scaffold, the axman waiting for me."

"To live with such dreadful uncertainty is no easy thing," he said, coming closer to her.

"I was in the Bell Tower, in a hideous room. The dampness seeped deep into my bones. It was always dark—the windows were painted—and I thought I should lose my mind until they allowed me to start walking outside. Seventy feet of sunshine, when there was any, but not even that could burn the dampness out of my bones."

He took her hand, rubbed it. "But you are warm now."

"Yes, but to keep that way it seems that I must send another queen to something worse than a damp cell."

Her eyes were so very different from Bess's. Equally

bright, equally captivating, but Bess's were more open, more inviting, and the realization of this saddened him. Elizabeth had to be guarded even with those she loved.

"I want to be of use to you," he said. "But there's little I can do other than listen. So talk to me, talk to me, my queen."

"I would have you call me something more dear."

"As would I." He felt a piercing disloyalty to Bess as he said this, pictured the flashing jealousy that crossed her face whenever Elizabeth pulled him into a corner so they might talk alone. "But you will not—"

"No. I won't. And I can't think about it now, Water." She looked strong again. "If I sign the death warrant, how will Mary's son react to his mother's execution? James would be my heir. He might decide he'd prefer to rule England now, instead of waiting for me to die."

"He signed the Treaty of Berwick, did he not? He's your ally."

"If I kill his mother, he might be less inclined to view himself as such. Although I do give him a generous pension." She sighed. "And what of the French? Mary's first husband was their king for a year before he died and they still consider her their queen. By executing her, I hand them a perfect excuse to join Spain against me."

"Possibly," he said.

She smiled, shook her head. "And Philip would undoubtedly be bent on revenge."

"Yet if you let her live . . ."

"I will always be in danger. I am not so void of judgment that I do not see my own peril."

"The country is rife with rumor," he said, admiring the brave confidence creeping into her eyes. "Just today I've heard stories of the Spanish already landing at Milford, the northern counties in revolt, and that London—contrary to all available evidence—is burning."

"Burning?"

"Yes. And Mary's escaped and heading north."

"I cannot allow this to continue. Yet what will people say when, for the safety of her life, a maiden queen could be content to spill the blood even of her own kinswoman?"

"Perhaps they will say that she preserved the peace of her country." He recognized the resolve in her eyes. "You've already decided to do it, haven't you?"

"Another plot has been uncovered, this one started by the French, on Mary's behalf, of course. They meant to poison me, though apparently argued over how, precisely, to do it. So, yes, I must sign the warrant. So why have I not?"

"It's that fear—that fear of being so mortal," he said.

"You understand me well."

"I've always tried."

"It means more to me than you can ever know." Their eyes met, level and calm, full of love.

"We mortals have many weaknesses," he said. "We feel

too much. Hurt too much. And all too soon, we die. But we do have the chance of love."

She closed her eyes. "Who taught you to say such things to me?"

"You did." He wished, despite his love for Bess—a love that filled his heart and was with him at every moment—that he could have Elizabeth. To win her love, to be hers, to be free to adore her—how could he not want that?

She nodded, eyes still closed. "Leave me now. What I must do, I must do alone."

Chapter 16

Mary's room was cold, but the complaint was a trivial one. They had brought her supper, but she'd long ago lost the desire to eat, and fed tidbits from the table to Geddon while she prayed, silently, to herself. She'd spent nearly three months consumed with uncertain anguish, knowing that she would die but not when. She'd written to Elizabeth, begging that her execution be expedited, but Paulet would not deliver the letter.

This was too long to prepare for death.

But tonight, when the door opened and she saw her jailer—drawn, gray, tired—relief swept through her body as she realized her waiting was over. "Your face tells me. It's decided."

"Tomorrow morning. At eight." Sir Amyas did her the courtesy of looking into her eyes as he spoke. She took a deep breath, trying to identify the feelings inside her. Relief, of course, but what else? She could not tell. She expected to be scared, but terror had not yet come, perhaps because her heart did not yet believe the waiting was over.

"I thank you for bringing such welcome news," she said. She looked at him and, for the first time since she'd met him, had no need to pretend to flirt or to feign piety. "I am very glad to leave a world in which I am not welcome."

"I'm— I'm sorry," he said.

"Do not apologize. There's nothing else left for me. I've known that for far too long. You were kind to me until you learned of my secret correspondence, and I can hardly fault you for being angry at me then."

"I will pray for your soul," he said, then bowed to her and left the room.

As soon as the door closed, Annette fell to the floor, wailing and sobbing. But her mistress stood perfectly still, showing no sign of distress, maintaining her regal bearing. "Don't cry," Mary said. "I mean to die in such a way that our cause will live forever." This would be her legacy, would bring her immortality. Nothing in her life would approach the vital importance of her death. And when it was over, there would be no more prisons, no more lies. She would have no task but to bathe in the glory of God.

SHE SPENT HER LAST night putting things in order, glad for the occupation. Sleep was impossible, not only because of anxiety that could not be kept at bay but because it seemed a terrible waste. She did not want to miss a single moment of consciousness now that there were so few left for her. She had already begun labeling everything: her last sunset, her last exchange with a previously unnoticed servant, the last time she would brush her hair. It all took on more significance than she felt it deserved, but she could not help herself.

Sitting at her table, she wrote a final letter to Elizabeth, holding the pen too tightly at first and breaking the quill. She sharpened another one and began again, the words coming quickly as she gave pardon to all her accusers and begged the queen to let her be buried in France. But at the end, she had harsh words for her cousin:

> *Accuse me not of presumption if, leaving this world and preparing myself for a better, I remind you will one day to give account of your charge in like manner as those who preceded you in it, and that my blood and the misery of my country will be remembered, wherefore from the earliest dawn of your comprehension we ought to dispose our minds to make things temporal yield to those of eternity.*

Satisfied, she signed the paper: "Your sister and cousin and wrongfully a prisoner." Her hand was shaking with anger at this woman who had refused to give her even the simple courtesy of a personal meeting, who had callously condemned her to death. She did not want to squander any of this night on hatred, but it was difficult to feel no ire when she thought of the English queen, smug in her palace, surrounded by sycophants. She sighed and prayed, prayed for the grace to forgive her, grace that would bring her peace on this final night of her life.

Next she set about dividing her few possessions among her loyal ladies and servants. There was little left to give, and as she tried to disperse it fairly, she found continual distraction in a single thought: she would not be alive at this time tomorrow. *She would not be alive.* Now she began to feel scared, terror creeping through every inch of her body. Did it matter who would wind up with her rosary? Who would get her prayer book? Her gold crucifix? Her embroidery? She told herself that it did, that it had to, and she wrote careful directions that she would leave behind, all the while knowing this was trivial when compared to the remainder of what was consuming her mind.

More letters came next, farewells to her friends—the few who remained—and then she set herself to the most painful task before her. The letter to her son, James. She broke down and wept thinking of him. She would forever picture him as the ten-month-old child she'd last seen at Stirling Castle in Scotland after she'd been forced to abdicate her throne. She remembered him, his head covered with fuzzy auburn hair, trying to pull himself to standing, his little hands clutching the side of a table. The polished wood was too slippery. He lost his grip and fell, crying as his head hit the floor. Mary had swooped him up in her arms and soothed him. She could still smell the warm, clean scent of him, feel his plump hands, hear his breath slow as she'd calmed him.

But that was twenty years ago, and she'd not been allowed to see him again. He had grown into a man without ever knowing his mother. She had no idea what he was like, what he'd been told about her, if he'd received any of the gifts she'd sent him when he was a child. Futile thoughts, especially now.

She penned one final letter, to Henri, King of France, younger brother of her first husband. "Royal brother," she began. ". . . I scorn death and vow that I meet it innocent of any crime, even if I were their subject. The Catholic faith and the assertion of my God-given right to the English crown are the two issues on which I am condemned, and yet I am not allowed to say that it is for the Catholic religion that I die, but for fear of interference with theirs."

This would do. This would be her legacy. She would be remembered not as a conspirator but as a martyr. She continued on, telling him, as she'd told Elizabeth, of her desire to be buried in France, knowing all the while that the English queen would do with her body whatever she wanted. And that was unlikely to be anything that would give Mary satisfaction. She signed this, her last letter, at two o'clock in the morning. Six more hours to go.

As she put down her pen, she tried not to think about the ax, not to wonder if she'd feel its strike, not to hope that her executioner would be quick. But to avoid such thoughts was impossible, and she began to feel as if she were drowning, and she welcomed it at the same time she abhorred it. Because to feel was to be alive—and any emotion, even a hideous one, was preferable to none. Still, she could not let herself come unhinged. So she prayed, and eventually the night that had seemed both interminable and far too brief ended.

The sun fought its way through thick gray clouds, and she heard familiar sounds as the castle's occupants started their ordinary routines. A stable door slammed sharply and horses neighed greetings to the boy bringing food to their stalls. Soft footsteps announced servants carrying water. Wheels crunched gravel on the drive. But today the wheels did not belong to merchants or other tradesmen. They carried coaches full of dignitaries arriving to witness the day's spectacle, to see the Queen of Scots die.

She watched at her window until her ladies came to help her dress. She did not admit them to the room at once, knowing that these were her last minutes alone. She gave herself a final gift: two minutes of absolute panic. She pictured the ax and its bloody work. She let desperation overwhelm her as she clutched her head, pulled her hair, screamed into her pillow. Her breath came with such rapid force that she grew dizzy, and she staggered, falling against the wall.

And then she forced it all away—the last real emotions she'd ever show. It was more difficult than anything she'd done before, but somehow she managed to stop her limbs from shaking, her muscles from twitching. She went to her mirror and smoothed her hair, splashed last night's water on her face, pressed a damp cloth against her eyes. She couldn't quite yet bring herself to let them in. She sat on the bed. Went to the window. Paced the room three times, all the while silently saying Hail Marys. And then, when she knew she could delay no longer, she opened the door, revealing to her ladies a vision of pious composure.

They did not give her the same. They wept, keened, begged her to find some way to escape.

"You must stop," she said, her voice perfectly even. "You must help me prepare." Still crying—but silently now—they helped her dress in the simple black gown Mary had chosen for the occasion.

Eight o'clock approached, and she heard heavy steps outside her door. It was time. They had come for her. No one spoke on the way to the great timbered hall of the castle, where a stage had been constructed in the center, surrounded by chairs, none of which was empty.

"Please help me mount this," she said to a servant as she approached the scaffold. "It is the last request I shall make of you." She walked with grace, her black gown flowing around her, auburn hair tied in a bunch. Her ladies were still weeping, no longer trying to hide their distress, but the Queen of Scots kept her dignity, her eyes flashing with anger only when she was offered the services of a Protestant minister. They would not give her a Catholic one.

The executioner stepped forward, prepared to remove her veil, but she moved away from him, not letting him touch her. Instead, her ladies came, took the veil, her jewelry, and unfastened her dress. As the gown fell to the ground, the spectators gasped. Underneath it, she wore a petticoat of dark red silk, the color of martyrdom.

Now her executioner knelt before her. "Forgiveness, Your Grace."

"I forgive you with all my heart, for now, I hope, you will make an end of all my troubles." One of her ladies, crying, fastened a handkerchief over Mary's eyes. The former queen knelt, put her head on the block. "Into Your hands, O Lord, I commend my spirit."

She stretched out her arms as a signal, praying that they would remain steady, that the horrible terror consuming her would not be evident. She could hear the man beside her moving, the sleeves of his shirt brushing against his sides as he raised his ax. And then a silent pause. She realized she was holding her breath and forced herself to draw air, knowing it would be her last.

The ax fell, but the blow was not enough to sever her head, so two more followed in rapid succession before the deed was done. The executioner bent to grab the bloody prize and hold it up for the crowd to see, but he did not realize he was gripping a wig. The head fell and rolled across the floor, revealing to all that Mary's hair was as sparse and gray as that of someone twenty years her senior.

It was a horrific sight and grew worse when people noticed the dead woman's skirts moving. Out from them crept her little dog, Geddon, whimpering and confused at the sight of his mistress's headless torso. He nudged the body with his nose and was soon covered in blood, whining. No one moved. At last, Annette stepped forward and took him in her arms, both of them crying at the loss of their lady.

PHILIP'S AMBASSADOR SENT WORD of the execution as soon as it had happened. Mary, Queen of Scotland and France, was with God, a glorious martyr. She'd gone in spectacular fashion, serving in death the faith she'd honored in life. If Philip's own work on earth were not so urgent, so crucial, he might have envied her this holy end. Martyrdom would never be his, but he could free the souls of England, return them to the true word of God. And his daughter, the infanta, would take her place on the throne.

He squeezed Isabella's hand as the sound of cheering crowds in the plaza outside the Escorial Palace jarred him from his meditation. Roaring voices united, chanting a single word, over and over: *War*. He had already prayed for Mary's soul, had greeted his people. Now he came in from the balcony and stood before his assembled ministers.

"All Christendom now knows I have just cause. Much as I hate war, it is now my sacred duty." His eyes shined bright. He looked down at the infanta, who was smoothing her doll's red hair. She would help him finish God's work. She would bring the souls of England to heaven.

At Whitehall, Elizabeth could hardly bear the pain consuming her. She had brought this agony on herself, and despite it having been the right thing—the only thing—to do, she was not at peace. She'd raged when her request that Sir Amyas Paulet quietly take care of Mary—under the guise of the Act of Association—had been refused. His response infuriated her: "God forbid that I should make so foul a shipwreck of my conscience or leave so great a blot to my poor posterity to shed blood without law or warrant." She would have loved to have thrown him in the Tower.

And now the bloody day had arrived, the last of her cousin's life. Elizabeth had risen before the sun, tried to sit, pray, contemplate, but was too agitated. She paced. She threw things. She screamed. Finally, she could stand it no more. She charged into the Presence Chamber, where the entire court was waiting for her.

"Stop it! Stop the execution! I demand it be done!" The courtiers had fallen silent as soon as she entered, and she could read the horror on their faces. It mattered not to her. They could think whatever they wanted. There was no controlling the emotions rioting in her.

"What are you waiting for?" She yelled louder. "I am your queen! I order you to have this stopped!"

No one stepped forward, no one was looking at her. They were staring at the floor, and she despised them all. She spun around.

"You disobey me?" Her voice was shrill. "I will banish you all from court. I will—"

She had not noticed Raleigh was in the room until he came close and stood next to her. She fell quiet, turned, and buried her head in her hands, hiding the tears flowing from her eyes as she breathed in the smell of tobacco smoke clinging to his clothes. She was still—but not for long. At eight o'clock—the time the ax was scheduled to fall on her cousin's neck—she cried out and sank to the ground, sobbing. Raleigh knelt on the floor and Bess came to her side, the two of them together supporting her in a single embrace.

She hardly knew how she'd passed the rest of the day. But as it grew dark, she regained her control and was herself again—serene—when Walsingham found her, alone, in the Privy Chamber. Her moods passed as quickly as they descended upon her.

"Forgive me," he said, on his knees, abasing himself before the queen. "In my weakness and my vanity, I have failed you."

"How have you failed me? What am I to forgive you for?"

"Philip of Spain is a God-fearing man. He cannot make war without just cause. He sent the Jesuit to kill a queen, but not you."

"Not me?" Confusion registered in her eyes.

"The Jesuit's mission was to draw Mary Stuart into the murder plot. He knew I was reading her every letter. He waited until she wrote the words that sealed her guilt."

"And I ordered her execution." Elizabeth spoke slowly. "I murdered God's anointed queen. And now God's most dutiful son makes holy war to punish me."

"Forgive me, Majesty. Let me go."

"No, Francis. I am no fool. I considered this possibility when I made my decision. I knew the danger my actions courted." Her voice was measured, steady, but began to reveal stronger emotion as anger filled her veins. "England has a God too," she said. "Let Philip do his worst. We'll see whose God is still standing at the end!"

Colorful prisms of light danced on the wall, split by the leaded glass of Raleigh's bedroom window. "I hate to think about the life we might have had together if our circumstances were different," Bess said. She was spending far too many afternoons in his bed at Durham House.

"Hate? Why?" he asked, lighting his pipe after he'd fluffed the pillows behind her.

"Because it's futile. We can't go on like this indefinitely."

"Why not?"

"We'll get caught or you'll get married or—"

He silenced her with a kiss. "I do not like the sadness in your eyes. Banish it." He reached to a table by the side of the bed, grabbing from it a sheaf of papers. "Here—a gift for you. A manuscript of a play by a new writer, Christopher Marlowe. It's called *Tamburlaine*."

"I've heard of this," she said, turning to her side and leaning on an elbow. "Margaret knows someone who saw it performed."

"I saw it performed. It was magnificent."

"You're trying to distract me," she said. "It's not working."

"Then I shall have to try harder."

She put a finger to his lips to stop him from kissing her. "No. I must tell you this. I fear that what we are doing will destroy us."

"You want to stop?" His voice was serious.

"Should we?" she asked.

"Of course we should. And the poor should have food and Spain should leave England alone."

"That does not make what we are doing right."

He took her face in his hands. "I love you, Bess. What makes this right is the fact that we were designed for each other, that we understand each other, that we need each other. I will never choose to walk away from you, whatever the cost. I don't want to hurt her any more than you do."

"Do you love her?"

"I do. I'm sorry if it hurts you."

"It doesn't, though I can't understand why." She sighed. "You love her, yet you will still come to me?"

"Forever. Even if we can never have more than these stolen hours. Forever, Bess."

ELIZABETH'S NIGHTS WERE TROUBLED, full of the horrors and pressures of planning for war. She craved privacy, solitude—two things unreachable, for even when she was alone, she knew droves of courtiers waited outside. She had gone to her bedchamber with a book, shutting the door on the supportive but irritating faces of her ladies-in-waiting. There was only one person she wanted to see. Walking back and forth in front of her window, she read aloud, knowing he would come as soon as her summons arrived, wishing she hadn't needed to ask.

"Think you that there is any certainty in the affairs of mankind, when you know that one swift hour can destroy the greatest among us?" She turned at the sound of the door opening. Seeing Raleigh, she held up the book. "Boethius."

"*The Consolation of Philosophy*," he said, coming to her side.

"Thank you for coming at this late hour." It felt good to be close to him. Safe. She closed the book and set it on the table next to her bed. "We're at war. Who knows when we'll meet again. If we'll meet again."

"May the Lord God preserve England's Queen." His formal tone, cold and impersonal, disappointed her.

"The same God in whose name Philip wages his holy

war. Philip is a righteous man, and righteous men love to destroy. They burn whole worlds to make them pure, and leave behind ashes."

"He'll not burn England."

"He may. His Armada is invincible, they say. If London falls, if I'm captured, then I'll have one more short walk to take. I'll climb the steps my mother climbed. And then—all over."

"Never." The strength—bordering on arrogance—of his voice brought a strange sort of comfort to her.

"Never?" She drew a deep breath. "It's night and my thoughts turn dark. Don't you ever think that one day, perhaps one day soon, you too will die?"

"The closer I come to death, the more I want to live. The hungrier I am for life," he said, a defiant gleam in his eyes.

"You're right, Water," she said, breaking her morbid mood. "We must live while we can."

"Why be afraid of tomorrow? Today's all we have, and all we know."

"Today. Tonight." Their gazes held steady.

"Now."

"I wish—" She stopped, couldn't say it.

"I've never known a woman like you," he said. She saw in his expression everything and knew that perhaps, this time, not giving herself fully had been a mistake.

"In some other time, in some other world, could you have loved me?" she asked.

"I know only one world. In this world, I have loved you."

Her smile was small, hesitant. "Then there's something you could do for me—something I've not known for a very long time—if you felt so inclined." He came closer as she spoke. "Something not to be spoken of afterward—to be forgotten—but just for now—" She lifted her head to his. "A kiss?"

He took her in his arms and brought his lips, cool and soft, to hers, forcing them apart. One kiss to hold all that might have been, all that could never be. When at last they parted, she turned away from him, head bowed, eyes still closed, the sweetness of the moment painted on her calm cheeks and smiling mouth.

"Thank you," she said. A perfect kiss could make even a war easier to bear.

Chapter 17

The outside of Lisbon Cathedral looked as much like a fortress as a church, and a crowd swarmed in front of it, its enthusiasm cresting in a ground-shaking roar as the royal procession passed. Carried at the front was a flag bearing an image of the Virgin Mary—the flag that would serve as the great Standard of the Armada. The king marched behind it, a somber figure leading a column of Spain's nobles into the cathedral, past the font at which St. Anthony was baptized and on to the altar, where an archbishop sprinkled it with holy water and made the sign of the cross over it.

"Exurge, domine et vindica causam tuam. Amen."

Philip knelt to kiss the newly blessed standard before it was thrust aloft again into the vast spaces of the nave, which, unlike the exterior, lacked nothing in ornate decoration. The congregation applauded and wept, ready for battle, confident of victory as music soared through the nave, echoing the triumphant emotions. Then all fell quiet and mass began.

The familiar ritual was like a heady stimulant, sending through his body sparks that brought with them enlightenment, clarity, purpose. He breathed deeply, drawing smoky incense into his lungs, reveling in the sweet spices as the rhythm of a Latin prayer pulsed. He soared with the choir as they began to sing a forceful series of *amens,* his voice louder and stronger than those around him. And when the mass was finished, he rose from his pew and led the procession to the harbor to bask in the glory of the Most Fortunate Armada.

The hundred and thirty ships, tall as castles, pulled against their anchors, the red crosses on their sails filling as the wind blew cold. Philip presented the standard to the Duke of Medina Sidonia, Don Alonso Perez de Guzman, commander of this most impressive fleet, and soon the standard was on his flagship. The triumphant cries of the assembled masses seemed deafening until they were drowned out entirely by the Armada's cannons firing a booming salute as the flag was hoisted into place, billowing among a forest of masts as ships filled the horizon.

It was an incomparable marvel—a masterful example of Spanish superiority. Not only would these ships wreak destruction on their puny English counterparts, the mere sight of them would drive stakes of fear through the enemy's heart. And all this—all of it—would bring glory to God.

Philip was pleased.

❧

All of England was shouting stories about the imminent arrival of the Spanish. Rumor said that three—no, four—some had heard as much as five—hundred ships were closing in on Dover. The army they carried was not only huge but full of savages, ready to kill every adult, both male and female, in England. And it was said that also on board were seven thousand Spanish wet nurses, who would suckle the newly orphaned children of Britain.

Not that England was unprepared. Immense chains had been stretched across the Thames, from Gravesend to Tilbury, to block approaching ships. Lord Howard, admiral of the English fleet, ordered Sir Francis Drake, the explorer, to patrol near Plymouth, and troops, raised daily, marched toward Tilbury, where they would build an encampment and wait for the enemy. Fear circulated but so did hubris and a brash desire to join battle and force Philip's lackeys from English soil.

At Whitehall, armed men marched through the corridors while servants hauled trolleys packed with valuables to be hidden away: paintings, porcelain, golden ornaments. Bess was in the midst of the commotion, looking for Raleigh, a dull pain in her chest. Quickly out of breath, she dodged soldiers and courtiers racing through the lengthy corridors, at last finding him across from the Guard Chamber. She hovered, waiting while he finished speaking to an earnest-looking soldier, then caught his attention and beckoned him to a secluded corner. He came at once, taking both her hands in his.

"Bess, I've been ordered to my ship—"

She stopped his mouth with one finger. "I'll be quick," she said, her heart pounding. "I have something to tell you. But I ask for nothing. Is that understood? Your life is your own. Nothing will change."

"What is this, Bess?"

Two court officials hurried by. She lowered her voice, wished for a moment that she didn't have to tell him. Wished for every impossible thing. "I'm—" She stopped, bit her lip, looked down, and touched her waist.

"You're pregnant?" he asked.

She nodded. "No one knows. My plans are made. I shall ask the queen for permission to leave court. I shall live quietly in the country with my child. The queen must know nothing."

He stared at her, his eyes full of shock, but pulled her closer. "Where will you go?"

"To my mother's house." She looked at the floor and realized she was already consumed with the grief of losing him. It felt as if the deepest parts of her had been savagely attacked, and the raw wounds pulled apart.

"Must you?"

"I'm a ward of the queen. I can't be courted by a man without her permission. I can't marry without her permission. As for having a child—" She fell silent as another official passed them.

"When will you leave?" he asked.

She hadn't expected him to ask her to stay. But that did not keep his simple question from cutting deeply. She swallowed hard. "As soon as I'm allowed."

She looked up at him and saw that he, too, was struggling. He pressed his hands to his forehead, closed his eyes, shifted his weight. "Am I not to see you again? What's to become of the child? Bess—"

"Hush!" His weakness gave her strength. She touched his lips. "We've no choice. You know it as well as I do."

"All I know is nothing's as it should be." He rested his forehead against hers, and the heat of his skin swallowed her.

"Please listen. You once said to me, 'Whatever I have to give, ask and it's yours.' Do you remember?"

"Of course I remember."

She could see in his eyes that he spoke the truth, that he would do anything for her, and she let herself wish, for the briefest moment, that their love did not have to be illicit, that they could give themselves freely and wholly to each other. But wishing that, even for an instant, did nothing but open her heart to more hurt. "I ask that you forget me. Go to your ship. Do your duty. Forget me."

"Do not ask that of me," he said.

"I have no choice."

"There is always a choice, Bess. Sometimes it's difficult.

Sometimes it hurts other people. But sometimes it's still right. Sometimes it's what must be."

"I cannot," she said. "I cannot do it to her."

He did not move his eyes from hers. "Bess . . ."

The queen's ladies rushed by, Margaret calling out on their way. "Bess! We're summoned."

"I'm coming," Bess said, then turned to Raleigh. "Goodbye." She nearly choked on the word, the pain of it unbearable. Her throat burned, her eyes ached, and every muscle in her body stiffened. She could not bring herself to look at him again, knowing that if she did, she'd throw herself in his arms. Against all her will and all her heart, she forced herself to turn away and ran down the hall.

THE PRIVY CHAMBER HAD been polluted by an oppressive tension since Mary Stuart's execution. All the members of Elizabeth's council felt her fury, but it was William Davison, a secretary, who received the bulk of it. It was he whom she'd sent to convince Paulet to get rid of Mary on his own, to spare the queen having to sign the death warrant. When Davison failed on that mission, she sent him to the Tower, threatening to hang him.

She hadn't followed through, of course, but she could see that her moods took a toll on her ministers. It was obvious when they were afraid of her—the way they slouched in their seats, spoke more quietly than usual. They should fear her; all their happiness, their success depended upon her favor, and she would not tolerate disloyalty. And disloyalty, she believed, included failing at what should have been a simple task, like that she'd given to Davison.

But now they sat around the table, united again, ready to address the Spanish threat.

"What is the condition of our fleet?" Elizabeth asked.

"I'd like more ships, Majesty," Lord Howard said.

"I understand this Armada Philip is building has ships the size of castles."

"Ships that will be difficult to maneuver," Howard said. "I don't think they can beat us."

"Of course they can't beat us," she said. It felt good to be in control again, to know that she would lead England to victory. She smiled at her men: Walsingham, Howard, Hatton, and Burghley. She was ready to listen to their advice.

"Bess!" Raleigh pulled her away from the other ladies as they left the hall after supper that night, headed to the queen's quarters for dancing. "I must speak with you."

"No," she said. "I can't. Please—"

"You cannot refuse me a conversation." His eyes pleaded. "Just talk to me." She closed her eyes and sighed but did not resist when he took her hand and led her outside, past walls of guards to an empty garden, flowers long since dead from frost. No one would see them here.

"What do you want?" she asked, eyes filling with tears. He was making this all so difficult. She wished he would go away, sail on his ship, never come back. If he did, in a hundred years or so, she might start to forget him.

"Marry me, Bess. Marry me."

"I can't. You know I can't. It's impossible."

"Nothing is impossible. Choices, remember? Difficult choices? You cannot ask me to leave you, to pretend we'd never met. You're my heart, Bess, and I will not let you escape from me."

"The queen will never give us permission," she said.

"So we'll do it secretly, tell no one. You'll go to the country to have the baby, just as you'd planned. But you won't be alone, Bess. You'll never be alone."

"Why? Why do this? Why not just go on as we are?"

"Because I need to know that you are mine, even if no one else can." He pulled her close, embraced her, kissed her neck. "Stay with me, love me, have me for your own."

She put her hand to his head, held it against her neck, felt his tangled curls. "I suppose we're risking no more than we already have."

"And gaining something far more dear than anything we could lose, even if we're discovered."

This made her laugh. "Really? More dear than your head? We'd soon find ourselves on the scaffold if the queen were to discover us."

"She didn't send Leicester to the scaffold when he married Lettice Knollys."

"She was in love with Leicester." A sigh. "And she's in

love with you. It makes it worse, don't you think? To think our lives are protected because she loves you?"

"No, I don't. She loves me, Bess, but she won't have me. Is it fair, then, for her to keep me from you?"

"Queens don't have to be fair."

"And when they're not fair, are we required to do their bidding when it hurts us?"

"Sometimes, yes."

"Not this time."

"If she would take it, would you give her everything? Or would you be here with me?" He buried his head deeper in her neck but said nothing. "You would go to her, wouldn't you?"

"I won't lie to you, Bess. I don't know. I don't know what I would do. But it doesn't matter—it's not our reality. Our reality is this—us, our child. I love you. Will you have me? Will you take my everything?"

Her breath was coming fast as she looked into his eyes. "I will. I will take your everything and give you mine in return." He kissed her, and all her fears disappeared. They'd come back, that she did not doubt, but she would always be able to recall the simple perfection of this moment.

Elizabeth's nightmares were getting worse, and Bess, who'd always been able to soothe her in the past, had been too distracted of late to be of much help. She'd noted the girl's pale face and sketchy appetite and worried, insisting that she drink foul-tasting tinctures daily, but they yielded little result. So now, when she needed her favorite friend, instead of calling for her to sleep next to her, she found herself alone, not trusting any of the others enough to let them see her so vulnerable.

Sleep did not come easy, and when at last it did, something—a sound, light, she knew not what—woke her in the night. She was frightened, the curtains of her bed pressing in, overwhelming her with claustrophobia. She flung them apart, only to find the shadows filling her room equally terrifying. They floated and dove with sinister movements and she screamed, no longer caring who saw or heard her.

"Air! I must have air!" Her servants rushed in, opening the windows. Guards appeared next, followed by ladies in their streaming nightgowns. Elizabeth took no heed of any of them. She leaned over the sill, drawing in a deep breath of night air while she watched the moon, all the while overwhelmed with the sensation that something terrible was about to happen.

Chapter 18

Escaping from the palace was more difficult than during Bess's previous nighttime adventures, but she and Margaret managed to slip past the guards without drawing questions. A boat was waiting for them near the privy stairs, and they climbed aboard and were quickly settled, sitting close together. Margaret dropped her head onto her friend's shoulder. "You're quite certain you want to do this?" she asked.

"There's nothing I want more," Bess said, heart racing, stomach tingling with nerves.

"You know there will be consequences."

"No one need learn what's happened."

"The baby, Bess. People will know."

"Eventually, yes, but perhaps by then . . ." Bess's voice trailed.

"By then the queen will have another favorite?" Margaret shook her head. "You know it's not that simple. She would never agree to let you marry him. Never. And if she finds out that you already have—"

"I know, Margaret, I know. But I adore him. He's everything to me. There's nothing I wouldn't risk to be with him."

"Sweet words, my friend, but romance doesn't translate so well to reality. Aren't you scared at all?"

"Of course I am. Terrified." Bess tugged at her lip. "He's taught me that some things are worth great risks." She reached for Margaret's hand. "You must be happy for me, if only for tonight."

"You know I wish you great joy. I just—"

"Stop there, please."

"Very well." Margaret gave her a smile, but it was forced and full of concern. "We will be happy tonight." The barge slowed as they approached the dock at Durham House and she saw Raleigh waiting for them. All anxiety flew from her when she looked at his handsome face and she began to believe that all would be well, that they would manage, somehow, to have each other without losing everything else. He gave her his hand, steadying her as she stepped off the swaying boat, then pulled her close.

"Forgive me. I can't wait any longer to taste you again," he whispered and kissed her lips, pulling back when Margaret clattered onto the dock. He gave each girl an arm and led them inside, through the courtyard and into the chapel, lit by the golden lights of hundreds of candles. A priest holding a worn copy of *The Book of Common Prayer* ushered them toward the altar, where they stood, facing each other. Margaret, their only witness, watched from the front pew.

The ceremony was short, as brief as church law would allow, but the air was heavy with emotion. They would be joined as man and wife but would not be able to live together, would have to continue to hide their love. Tonight, though, none of this mattered. Tonight, she would drown in his eyes and pretend that they would not be torn apart in the morning.

". . . with my body I thee worship, and with all my worldly goods I thee endow," he said, taking her hand.

He placed a ring on her left thumb. "In the name of the Father—"

He moved the ring to her forefinger. "And of the Son—"

To her middle finger. "And of the Holy Spirit."

Finally to her ring finger. "Amen."

Far to the south, the sun was rising over the English Channel, bursting through gathering clouds to dapple the rough water with sparkling diamonds. There was nothing else to see in any direction, only gray water, churning as if in preparation for a storm. But then, far off on the horizon, came a ghost of movement: dark shapes rocking in the waves. First a handful, then enough to stretch as far as the eye could see. No one on shore could see them yet. The sentries would still be staring idly, bored. But they'd know soon enough: the Armada was coming.

❧

In the center of Whitehall Palace, behind thick oak doors guarded by no fewer than two dozen well-armed men, stood the room in which Elizabeth was planning her war. Battle with Spain had been inevitable—the skirmishes already fought in ports and in the New World and the animosity between the two countries' religious establishments were not going to be peacefully resolved. As much as she hated that it had come to this, she had to admit that it had allowed her to redirect the anger she'd felt at her advisors, following Mary Stuart's execution.

All at once, she had the delicious feeling that she was standing on the precipice of a new era.

A magnificent map of Europe was inlaid on the floor, with model ships placed on it to depict the English and Spanish fleets, and still more maps covered the table standing in the center of the room. Elizabeth, imperious, stood tall, back straight, voice strong as she addressed Lord Howard, Hatton, Walsingham, and Burghley.

"This Spanish Armada is at sea, carrying an army of ten thousand men." She motioned to the map. "The Duke of Parma's fifteen thousand men are marching on Calais. At Tilbury, we have four thousand men." Parma, who commanded the superbly equipped Army of Flanders stationed in the Spanish Netherlands, could reach the English coast in very little time once he'd made it to Calais.

"Parma's army plans to cross the Channel in barges, under the protection of the Spanish fleet," Walsingham said.

"But as yet they don't have enough barges at Calais. We have a little time."

"That is so." Walsingham smiled, surprise in his eyes. She'd had every intention of shocking him with this information and was pleased to see she'd succeeded. "If the Spanish fleet reaches Calais in strength, the combined armies will be beyond our power to resist."

"Therefore," the queen continued, "the Spanish fleet will not reach Calais."

Lord Howard stepped forward. "Majesty, this Armada is three times greater than our fleet. We must be prepared for the worst. The court must leave London."

"I will leave London, Lord Howard," she said. "I will go to Tilbury. I will join my army."

"Do you think that's wise?" Burghley asked.

"I think it is necessary. I'm their leader, their queen. I must go to them. Unless you'd prefer I take up residence on one of our ships? Perhaps I could load cannons during the battle?" She was filled with satisfaction, knowing she was once again in control. The meeting finished, she walked briskly through the palace's public rooms to her quarters, Walsingham by her side, her entourage trailing behind.

"How did you know about the numbers of the Dutch barges, Majesty?" he asked. "I don't recall supplying you with that information."

"You may observe, Walsingham, that I don't see my way with only one eye. Nor do I hop along on only one leg. Why then would I rely on only one source of information?" She swept into her private rooms, her ladies jumping up in haste. She looked at them all, then turned to Margaret. "Where's Bess?"

"You're dull today," Elizabeth said. She and Raleigh had been playing chess. He'd let her win, not out of respect for her position but due to lack of attention, and she did not like it. "Is something wrong?"

"No, Majesty. I'm tired, that's all."

"I suppose you don't want to go for a walk then? The gardens are finally all in bloom."

"If you'd like, we can."

"I thought we could go to Windsor tomorrow and ride. What say you to that?"

"I am, as always, at your disposal."

She watched his face as he spoke, trying to read his emotions, but she could uncover nothing save an awkwardness she'd not before seen in him. "Have I done something to offend you?"

He grinned, but there was no heart in it. "Of course not. Shall we go outside? Show me your garden."

"No," she said. "I'd rather stay here and read. Why don't you go alone? Your mind is clearly elsewhere."

He didn't argue, didn't protest, only kissed her hand, bowed, and backed out of the room. And when he was gone, she leaned forward, resting her elbows on her knees, and buried her face in her hands. Her entire body started to ache as her head throbbed and her stomach turned. Something had gone wrong, desperately wrong. He was no longer with her, she could feel it, and she wanted to know where he had gone.

"Majesty?" The door opened and Walsingham stuck his head into the room. "There's something I think we ought to discuss. May I enter?"

She waved him in and forced herself to sit up straight and dignified. As soon as he began to talk, she no longer had to expend energy to appear regal. Anger filled her and a powerful queen took the place of the hurt woman that had been in the room. She knew exactly what she needed to do.

Chapter 19

Elizabeth had been sequestered in her study for more than an hour, questioning the ladies of the Privy Chamber, one after another in turn. Outside, in the atrium, courtiers sat in nervous silence. They dared whisper only when the queen's voice rose to a shout, audible even through the thick stone walls. Palpable tension did not make for easy companionship. The ladies looked at each other with accusing eyes, trying to determine who among them had brought on this rage. They all gasped when Margaret stumbled from the room in tears and ran out of the atrium without a word to anyone. No one dared go after her.

Some minutes later, the heavy doors flew open and Elizabeth stormed out, yelling, her face crimson, her voice shaking. She had suspected but never dreamed they would dare do this to her—humiliate her, betray her. It was beyond unacceptable. "Bess! Bess Throckmorton!"

Bess was sitting alone at the far end of the room, keeping her face down, not joining in the quiet gossip. At the sight of the queen, she rose. "Here, my lady." There was a tone of resignation in her voice, and the queen scowled, not caring who saw her boiling rage as the girl walked toward her. Hardly a breath was drawn in the atrium. No one dared speak, not that Elizabeth minded. They should never forget that she was their queen, that they were all here only because of her goodwill, should remember that she could destroy any of them in an instant. Her hands were shaking and she could not will them to stop, so she clenched them together in front of her. Once Bess had reached her, she slapped her, then smacked the side of her head.

"How dare you! You slut! You whore! Is it true? You dare to have secrets from me? Is it true? Do you deny it?" Bess stood, trembling hands over her face, saying nothing. Her silence further infuriated the queen. Elizabeth clenched her fists, her nails digging into her palms and drawing blood. "Tell me! Are you married? Are you with child? Are you with child?"

Bess lowered her hands and slowly looked up at the queen. "Yes, my lady." Her voice was weak but steady. Elizabeth thought she might collapse, the pain was that great. It started in her head and traveled through her body at a rate too fast to understand. Fury and hurt were unhappy companions, each vying for her full attention, but fury quickly won the battle, demanding to be heard.

"Slut! Whore! Traitress!" she screeched. "I am your queen! You ask my permission before you rut—before you marry—before you breed! My bitches wear my collars. Do you hear me? How dare you be with child?"

Walsingham stepped forward and reached for her. "Majesty, please! Dignity—mercy—"

Eyes blazing, she turned on him and pushed his hand away. How dare he? How dare any of them? She ground her teeth and only barely stopped herself from stamping her foot. "This is no time for mercy. That's what you said to me. I don't forget. But you showed mercy, Walsingham. Go to your traitor brother and leave me to my business." He blanched as she went back to berating Bess. "Is it *his* child? Tell me! Say it! Is the child his? Tell me! Say it! *Is it his?*"

"Yes, my lady." Bess was calm, dignified. "It is my husband's child." She was not looking at the queen but beyond her.

Elizabeth forced out a hard breath, the pressure in her head building at the outrage that she did not have the girl's full attention. She turned to see what had caught Bess's eye. Raleigh stood across the room, arms folded, eyes sad, watching. The sight of him struck her like no assassin's bullet could have. Shame and embarrassment mingled with her anger, and she would have liked nothing better than to run him through with a sword. But she had her wits about her enough to note that it was good there was not one readily at hand.

His voice was rough, low, barely audible. "This is not the queen I love and serve." He met Elizabeth's stare, his gaze unflinching, and she felt the madness draining out of her. Her fury remained, burning in her throat and stomach, but she controlled it, focused it, replaced its outward appearance with a mask of regal calm.

"You have seduced a lady under my care," she said, wishing she could bury this hurt, wishing she'd better protected her heart. "You have married without my consent. These are offenses punishable by law." She turned to Walsingham. "Arrest him."

She turned on her heel and disappeared into her study, the thud of the solid door as she slammed it echoing behind her. She put her hands, shaking, on her desk and lowered her head. Her lungs were paralyzed; she could not breathe. She dropped onto the floor, pulled her knees to her chest, and sobbed.

On the very tip of England, the Cornish coast, a young man stood in a watchtower. He'd been there for weeks, doing his best to maintain focus, to keep his eyes on the far-off horizon. It was a deadly dull post. No enemy ships ever passed him, and the ocean was starting to blur. The previous day he'd caught himself falling asleep, so this morning he'd brought with him a knife and a piece of wood and had set to carving it, promising himself that he'd be sure to look up every few minutes.

He'd heard all the stories about the Armada, about the

King of Spain—the Demon of the South, as he was called. They said he'd told a man condemned by the Inquisition that if his own son, the prince, were guilty of heresy, he would lead him with his own hands to the stake.

He rolled his shoulders, rocked his head back and forth, and turned his attention to the wood in front of him. But as he raised his knife, something caught the corner of his eye. The blade and wood clattered to the ground as he stared at the sea. Over the rim of the world appeared the long line of the Spanish fleet, a floating wall, black and menacing.

He raced down the steps of the tower, lit a bundle of sticks, and thrust them again and again into the beacon that stood nearby. As it caught fire, flames rising into the sky, he watched and soon saw a second beacon erupt on the next headland. Then a third on the next, and a fourth, and a fifth, until the line of fire stretched the entire length of the coast, warning all of Britain.

It was time. The queen must be informed at once.

"MAJESTY . . ." WALSINGHAM WAS being hesitant with her. He'd been treating her like a wounded bird for three days. It was unbearable.

"Say what you mean to, old man," she said, blue eyes flashing. They were rimmed with red, and she knew that although none of her courtiers would dare comment—let alone make an empty gesture of sympathy—she despised the fact that her heartbreak was obvious.

"It is perhaps not wise to lose control of your temper in such a fashion. Gossip, you know—"

"I have dealt with gossips from the time I was a girl. You would have me tolerate betrayal? Deceit? Lies? From a Lady of the Privy Chamber? The rules are clear, Moor. None of my ladies may allow a gentleman to court her without my express permission. You would have me make exception to this? Because I liked Bess? Because I liked Raleigh?" *Liked* Raleigh? She had loved him. *Loved* him. And for what? She hated the very sound of their names.

"No, Majesty. I would have you chastise the guilty parties in private. I would have you show nothing to the court but your serene, graceful self."

"Let them see me for who I am. Let them fear my anger." A queen should not have to contend with such treatment. She wondered how Raleigh liked the Tower and doubted that his accommodations there could be uncomfortable enough.

The other members of the Privy Council had hung back during this conversation, keeping eyes averted and faces turned. Elizabeth spun around, looking toward them, opening her mouth to say something and then stopping. She flew to the window. Outside it, the last of the warning beacons, the one within view of Whitehall burst into flames, and her heart raced. The Armada. All pettiness dropped away, and great calm centered itself in the core of her chest. She was again focused on her country, her people. This was what it meant to be a queen. England would always matter more than the trivial concerns of a human heart.

"So it begins," she said as excitement and delicious anticipation worked their way into her soul. "Gentlemen, our ships sail in English waters. Our armies stand on English soil. We will not be defeated. Believe me: I am England."

❧

"YOU SEE, IT'S NOT so bad," Raleigh said as Bess looked woefully around his room in the Tower of London. "It's small, granted, but I don't plan on doing much entertaining, and it's furnished adequately for a man of my station."

"How can you joke?" she asked. "It's dreadful."

"Not at all. There aren't even bars on the windows, and the guards let me walk outside when the weather's good. I'd expected much worse." And before he could stop himself, he rubbed his neck, glad his head was still attached. Bess reached for him, put her hand on top of his.

"I've found rooms nearby. The baby and I will be comfortable there."

"You are well, Bess?"

"Not so well without you." She looked at the floor and he saw a tear drop from her cheek.

"We must make the best of it," he said, looking at her face and memorizing every inch of it. "Do not be sad. We knew this could happen."

"I'm afraid," she said.

"Don't be." He pulled her onto his lap. "If the queen were

going to execute me, she'd have already done it. All there is to do is to remain patient and pray that eventually she releases me. But in the meantime, I cannot have you sad."

"What would you have me do?"

"Entertain me. The only good thing about prison is that the doors are locked, and the guards have promised not to open mine until you knock to signal that you're ready to leave."

"I'm not sure I'm capable of entertainment."

"I think you are." He kissed her, slowly, savoring the taste of her. "If my stay here is to be of some duration, I wonder if I could perhaps convince my jailers to move me to larger quarters and have you with me. Would you live with me in the Tower, Bess?"

"I would live with you anywhere," she said, returning his kisses. Jail, she soon found out, was not quite so dreadful as she'd been led to believe.

ELIZABETH FELT BETTER—SLIGHTLY—THE MOMENT the boat glided through the dark water. She was completely disenchanted with her courtiers, everyone at Whitehall. They scattered out of her way, afraid of her mood, when she approached. Walsingham and Burghley kept telling her to be calm, and her Privy Councilors all stopped talking when she entered the room. It was unbearable. So, she'd started to play the game, to put on an air of easy grace, to hide her anger. But she felt no need to keep anything from John Dee.

Hiding something from a man of his psychic abilities would be a futile effort, or so she told herself, glad for the excuse to not check her emotions.

When she arrived at his dock in Mortlake, she'd stormed into the house, not waiting to be announced, hardly waiting for the door to be opened, and stood before him, alone, full of anger and confusion.

"Majesty, this is a surprise."

She glared at him. "The fall of an empire, you told me," she said, prowling through his cluttered rooms, picking up instruments that looked interesting, then dropping them back down almost at once. "Why do I begin to feel like poor King Croesus? Who took at face value the words of the Oracle of Delphi?"

"You know your Herodotus. Excellent. But as I already told you, prophecy is an art, not a science."

"The Pythia told Croesus that if he crossed the Halys River, a great empire would be brought down. She did not mention that the empire was his, not the Persians'."

"Croesus should have considered the option," Dee said. "One can't find fault in the Pythia's words."

"I will not stand for clouded words. So, tell me: Did you mean the English empire? Because by God, England will not fall while I am queen. If that's your prophecy, sir, prophesy again."

"You want me to tell Your Majesty only what Your Majesty chooses to hear?" Dee asked.

"I will not be a toy of the fates. Have I not faced an assassin's bullet and lived?" She saw puzzlement in his eyes and did not like it. She sighed and felt the stabbing pain return to her stomach just as the seeds of a headache formed at the base of her neck. "Just tell me there's no certainty. The shadows of ghosts, you said. Any outcome is possible. Give me hope."

"The forces that shape the world are greater than all of us, Majesty. How can I promise you that they'll conspire in your favor, even though you are the queen?" he asked. "But this much I know. When the storm breaks, each man acts in accordance with his own nature. Some are dumb with terror. Some flee. Some hide. And some spread their wings like eagles and soar on the wind."

Elizabeth drew herself up. She knew her nature well, and it was noble. She'd made the mistake—again—of loving a man, of putting her faith in friends. It was not the path upon which God had placed her. Her heart was nothing more than a human flaw, and she must learn to control it, ignore it. She'd been made for England, for her people, to lead them and protect them. To bring them glory. She had to see and believe and feel that these betrayals that made her suffer in her very core were nothing but petty concerns when compared with the duty she owed her country. She would rise above it, never think of it again. She closed her eyes and banished the pain from her heart.

"You're a wise man, Dr. Dee."

"And you, madam, are a very great lady."

RALEIGH HEARD KEYS CLANGING outside his door before it swung open and the guard admitted a servant carrying his dinner on a tray. "Excellent," Raleigh said. "I'm famished and your food is not so bad. All things considered, this lodging is no worse than some I've taken on my own."

The servant did not reply.

"But the days are beginning to grow tedious. I think that should my stay here be a long one, I'll have to find something to occupy my time. Perhaps I'll write a book. A history of the world. How far do you think I could get before returning to the queen's good graces?"

"I know not, sir," the servant answered.

"Any letter from my wife today?"

"Not yet."

Bess wrote to him every day and visited as often as his jailers would allow. He missed her more than should have been possible, missed her even before she'd left when she came to him here. All he wanted was to have her back again, but he would have to wait, and waiting was something he despised. He blew out a sigh, changed the subject. "What news comes from the coast? Is the fleet at sea?"

"Yes, sir. May God preserve them."

"Who's in command?"

"Lord Howard and Sir Francis Drake, sir. That's all I know."

"England is in good hands," he said, wishing he was with them. The memory of spraying salt and endless sea taunted him. He rubbed his hands, which were growing soft, losing their calluses, and he thought of the feeling of rough ropes raising sails.

"As you say, sir." The servant bowed and left the room, the click of the key in the lock following quickly.

Raleigh abandoned his food and stepped to the window, looked out over Tower Green. Would Elizabeth spare him? Or would his life end here? The flip confidence he showed Bess when she came to him was not entirely sincere. He fell to his knees and prayed that God would help him find his way back to his wife and to the fleet.

Chapter 20

The Spanish ensign streamed from the masts of every ship, its yellow crosses on red backgrounds bright against the white cliffs of Dover, so close they seemed to have already been planted on shore. It was a daunting sight—but more so from a distance than from the decks of the massive ships. The English were preparing for a naval battle, but the Armada was not as strong as suspected.

The ships were not so well armed as they might have been, and before they'd set sail, desertion and disease had run through the sailors, forcing the Duke of Medina Sidonia to round up any men he could find. Supplies were short, food spoiled, and the duke had heard too many warnings of disaster from noted astrologers. He'd been seasick almost from the moment they'd left Lisbon, and so far, their mission had met with nothing that even approximated glory.

But he did not despair. Before they set sail, a simple friar had come to him to assure him God would be with them on their most holy crusade. And his words were the most sincere Medina Sidonia had ever heard.

He chose to believe them.

Storms had battered the great fleet on its journey to England, and the ships had suffered. Not all of them were new—some were converted merchant vessels, and not all were in the best of shape. Much would depend on Parma and his army, on the invasion, on the Armada serving more as support than an attacking force.

A small skiff pulled up alongside Medina Sidonia's ship, and a royal messenger scrambled up the side, bringing a letter from the king. Philip told him that in Spain, masses were being said almost continually, saints petitioned—the entire country was at prayer. The world was waiting for this victory, and God would not allow His mission to fail.

THE ENGLISH FLEET HAD sailed from Plymouth, and all that the people in London could do was pray. Elizabeth had decided to go to St. Paul's, away from the palace, closer to her subjects, needing to be buoyed by their adoration, walking slower than was her habit, carrying herself tall. Her entourage was heavily armed, soldiers carrying glittering weapons, their boots thudding and shields clanking as they marched beside her. Two thousand men protected her, and although she appreciated their devotion, she wondered if the country would not be better served by having them fight with the army.

The Ladies of the Privy Chamber had become more obsequious than ever since she'd ejected Bess from court, each hoping to become the queen's new favorite. They brought her sweets, shoes, books, and jewelry, all of which left her singularly unimpressed. She was beginning to despise the disposable nature of humans: lose one, replace with another. It did not feel right. She did not want a new companion.

Bess, she'd been told, had taken up residence near the Tower, wanting to be near her husband, a fact Elizabeth found profoundly irritating. Raleigh and his wife—she hated the sound of the word—should have prostrated themselves before her, should have begged for forgiveness. That they'd gone quietly was nothing short of infuriating. Infuriating and heartbreaking and she would fill the void in her chest left by them not with someone else but with ballast of stone. Philip's Armada could not have come at a better time. She was as grateful for the distraction it brought as she was terrified by it.

Elizabeth opened her eyes wide as they adjusted to the dim light, not missing at all the bright scrutiny of the sun. She pulled the cathedral's cool, musty air deep into her lungs as she focused her not inconsiderable intelligence, preparing herself. She already had the unmitigated support of her people; now was the time to rally them to action. She began giving orders.

"The bells are to ring in every church in the land. Laborers are to leave the fields and take up arms. The harvest must wait." She needed all men capable of fighting to join the troops already at Tilbury. "Release all prisoners. England is their country too."

She paused and closed her eyes at an unwelcome feeling of sadness. Raleigh was a skilled sailor, an experienced fighter, someone who could motivate his men and convince them to follow him anywhere. After a long sigh, she opened her eyes and turned, searching for and finding Walsingham. "Release Raleigh. He is forgiven . . . As I too pray to be forgiven."

"Very good, Majesty," Walsingham said, then dropped his voice so that only she could hear. "A difficult decision, I know, but the right one."

She gave him a small smile. "Leave me, all of you."

Her entourage disappeared from the nave—all but a grim-looking contingent of guards—the rest would be waiting to descend upon her the moment she stepped back outside. She walked to the altar and sank to her knees as a sublime feeling of confidence washed over her. The sun struggled through stained glass, and colored light danced on the stone floor. She raised her eyes to the window and decided that today she would not bow her head when she prayed.

News did not travel as quickly as he would have liked—a fact that filled Philip with frustration that made him feel as if his muscles would burst through his skin. Now, at long last, messages had arrived, but they were not at all what he had expected.

"When will they land in England?" He fingered a gold crucifix as he spoke.

"Communication has been difficult, Majesty. The duke is doing his best—"

"That is not acceptable." The king interrupted his minister with such force that the man prostrated himself in front of him. "I want news of invasion. Of success. Of souls returned to the true church."

"There was a delay—a temporary one. Parma was not ready. They had to wait six days for the army. But they will be on their way soon, Majesty." Parma, superior to every other general in Europe, would make up time as soon as they'd landed. His men, the Blackbeards, were seasoned veterans who would be able to crush the ill-prepared English army in a matter of hours. No one—not even the English—could doubt that.

"God rewards patience." Philip closed his eyes and prayed that God would give him patience, much more patience than he felt now. It was so hard to temper emotions, control anxious thoughts, when he was waiting for this great work to be done. Part of him wanted to command a ship himself, sail with the Armada, but he knew his place was here, with his people, his priests, praying.

He rose and stalked through the palace's lengthy corridors, sending courtiers and servants scurrying out of his way. When he reached his cell, the light from a single candle flickered in the plain space, as the chant of monks, warlike in its rhythm, drifted to him as he murmured his own prayer. "*Tu es Deus qui facis mirabilia solus. Notam fecisti in gentibus virtutem tuam . . .*"

THE ENGLISH ARMY WAS far from the finest in Europe. It included few professional soldiers, the bulk of its infantry made up of volunteers who knew better how to herd sheep than fight a battle. The officers did their best to rally the men's spirits, but though no one dared say it aloud, the general consensus was that it was essential the fleet keep the Armada from landing its invasion force.

A hasty camp had gone up at Tilbury, where Robert Dudley, in his new capacity as Lord Steward Her Majesty's Lieutenant Against Foreign Invasion, organized the men. Not everyone was pleased to see Leicester back in the queen's good grace. Elizabeth had placed him in charge of English forces sent to the Netherlands, and during his tenure there, Leicester had accepted the position of Supreme Governorship of the United Provinces offered by the Dutch Estates. The queen was furious, more so than she had ever been with him, and threatened to recall him, but her ministers managed to placate her, convincing her to let him remain.

Before long, she'd forgiven him, and if others had not—or were jealous because of the favor bestowed on him by his regal friend—Elizabeth did not care. She had no interest in the opinion of gossips.

Despite all that had passed between them over the

years—all the times he'd disappointed her—she knew he would always be dear to her. And to see him now, with the pain of Raleigh's betrayal so raw, would feel like coming home to familiar arms after too long away.

She had traveled from London on the royal barge and made a great spectacle of her arrival. Cannons fired a salute, and she paraded through the camp with a fife and drum corps. As soon as she'd stepped off her barge, she could hear nothing but Leicester's sweet voice.

"Majesty," he said.

"Eyes," she said, his nickname feeling good on her lips.

"It's been far too long."

"Yes." She had not decided yet how to react to him. She'd wanted to be distant but, as always in the past, found herself incapable of keeping her heart away from him.

"Still mad?" he asked.

"About what? Your deceitful marriage? Your travesties in the Netherlands? The appalling condition of my army?"

"I've missed you," he said.

"You expect my forgiveness to come too easily."

"Not at all. I've not slept for three nights worrying what you would say when you saw me."

"Would that I had executed you for treason when I had the chance." She could feel her eyes sparkling.

"You never had the chance. I wasn't guilty." He took her by the arm and spoke quietly. "I suppose we must play queen and her general now. But know that I'd much rather sit somewhere quiet and talk."

"We're in an army camp, Eyes. There's nowhere quiet to sit." She felt good seeing him, bantering with him. He looked much older than she'd expected—she'd heard rumors that he'd been ill, and his gaunt face suggested this was true. Did he look at her and begin to see her age, too? "Help me onto my horse."

He did, and then led the animal himself, holding the reins while she rode, an ocean of ragtag soldiers parting in front of her. The men had been soaked by rain before the arrival of the queen's party and were covered with mud, as was the entire encampment. They were suitably awestruck to find themselves so close to her, and she was pleased with her army, knowing, as she watched her army fall to its knees before her, that her infantry adored her.

"What news, Lids?" she asked, sitting down as Lord Hatton, breathing hard and clutching papers to his chest, rushed into the tent that Leicester had erected in anticipation of her visit.

"The enemy has been engaged, Majesty," he said. "A brave action. Two ships lost."

"With what gain?" Elizabeth asked.

"The enemy continues to advance."

"They must be stopped," she said, and rose from her seat, stood in the doorway of the tent, and looked out at the camp before her. The news had spread quickly: there was no joy to be seen in any direction. No one was singing; there was none of the ribald humor one expected from soldiers. All she heard was hushed voices, nervous murmurs, the sound of swords being ground against sharpening stones. A somber mood had settled like a disastrous fog.

Raleigh couldn't stop kissing her. Not that it mattered. He wouldn't have, even if he could.

"I can't believe she let you go," Bess said, her face flushed, eyes bright, stomach growing larger by the day.

"Nor can I. I suppose she thought she had no choice."

"We both know there's always a choice," she said, pulling him down on top of her.

"I can't stay, Bess, I have to go to the fleet."

She blew out a long breath. "I expected that. Another choice."

"Yes, it is. The right choice."

"Of course." She smiled at him, but he could feel her start to tremble in his arms, could see the fear behind her eyes. "You will come back to me, though?"

"Where else would I go? The Tower wasn't *that* comfortable," he said.

"You know what I mean. Promise me. Promise you won't leave me. That I won't lose you. I can't bear so many nights afraid, worrying that you'll be gone forever."

"I promise," he said and kissed her eyelids, her chin, every inch of her face. "I'll bring you glory and stars and every good thing when I return."

"Safe. I only want you safe. The stars aren't necessary."

"But you'll have them just the same," he said, silently praying that his words weren't lies, that he would come back, that he would see his child, that he would hold Bess again.

"Swear it," she said.

"I swear I will come home to you."

THE *Ark Royal*, FLAGSHIP of the English fleet, commanded by Lord Howard of Effingham, was an impressive vessel. Raleigh knew it well. A hundred feet long, nimble and strong, the galleon carried forty-four guns and had been built for him, before his fall from the queen's graces. From his cell in the Tower, he'd offered the ship for service, and Elizabeth had bought it from him at once. Whether he'd ever receive payment remained to be seen, but that was no concern of his. Not now, when he was standing on her bow as Spanish cannons shook the air around him.

Flashes of fire lit the deck, and he quickly assessed the situation around him. The ships of the Armada lumbered at a clumsy and slow pace, but their hulls were strong. The fight would be difficult but must be won. To let Parma's army slip through to shore would be nothing short of a disaster. He watched a volley of cannon fire from the *Ark Royal* batter the side of something that looked more like a merchant vessel than a warship. The shot struck its mark and the Spanish ship heaved to port.

Satisfied, Raleigh turned and headed to Howard's cabin in the sterncastle, where he found Sir Francis Drake arguing with the admiral.

"Attack again," Drake said. "We must attack. What choice do we have?" Drake, who had earned his knighthood after circumnavigating the world in his ship the *Golden Hinde*—the first man in England to accomplish such a feat—was no stranger to fighting the Spanish. With a fleet of nearly thirty ships, he'd gone to the New World to attack Philip's settlements there—revenge for a Spanish embargo that had paralyzed English exploration. He'd reopened America to his country and done a fine job of angering Philip in the process.

Howard shook his head. "We're outgunned. We're losing too many ships."

"We have to break their formation," Raleigh said, motioning to the chart.

Drake nodded. "Our ships may be smaller, but they're faster."

"I tell you, we're outgunned." Howard met Drake's eyes.

"I'm experienced in such things," Drake said. The queen had let her golden knight convince her to attack the Spanish port of Cádiz the previous year, and he'd managed to destroy twenty-five ships and capture a fortune in cargo, all the while modestly claiming only to have "singed the King of Spain's beard." "I've never served with better men or more gallant minds than those gathered here, voluntarily, to put their hands and hearts into the finishing of this great piece of work. We can do it."

"Do you want to lose the whole fleet?" Howard asked.

"God is with us," Drake said.

"Break their formation and we have a chance," Raleigh said.

"How?" Howard's eyes bled skepticism. "We can't get near them."

Raleigh's eyes danced. "There's one way."

Chapter 21

An air of mounting anxiety circulated through Tilbury. Soldiers congregated outside their tents, speaking in concerned whispers, sharpening their pikes, offering quiet prayers. Their ranks had swelled to close to seventeen thousand, and another twenty were at the ready in the maritime counties. Still, the mood in the queen's tent was bleak. Numbers alone could not make up for lack of experience.

"The Spanish are barely a day away, Majesty," Hatton said. "If they've got Parma's army and manage to land . . ."

Walsingham's face was dark. "It would be wise to withdraw to safer ground."

"My army will defend me." Elizabeth felt nothing but confidence.

"I beg you to appreciate the gravity of the situation, Majesty," Hatton said. "There is very little time."

Calm and defiant, she turned to him. "Then we must act. I know what to do. Leave me."

"Majesty—" Walsingham started.

"Now. Go." As she expelled them from her tent, she called for the handful of ladies she'd brought with her.

Margaret poked her head into the tent first and was quickly followed by three others. "How can we be of service?" she asked.

"It is time for me to become a vision of inspiration," Elizabeth said. "You must make me a warrior queen—Hippolyta or Boudica."

First, they removed her dark blue gown and replaced it with one cut from flowing white satin. They brushed her long red hair until it shone and left it hanging down her back, then turned their attention to the armor she'd brought with her. Now she would become Athena.

They strapped on the glistening silver breastplate, pulling up her lace collar to peek through the top, then slipped on her gauntlets. She tested them, slowly bending her elbows, the jointed metal moving more smoothly than she'd expected. In the back, they attached a long cape fashioned from a pale, rich brocade heavily embroidered in gold.

"Majesty, you exude strength," Margaret said, handing her a helmet with a tall, white plume.

"Call for Leicester," she ordered.

He arrived almost at once and dropped to one knee at the sight of her, his head bowed. "I am proud to call you my queen," he said.

"Prepare my horse, Eyes, and an honor guard. I want to rally my troops."

Soon there was a new sound in the camp: a low, distant rhythm, the beat of an army on the march, an army advancing amid an array of banners and flags. And in the center, her silver armor flashing, Elizabeth sat, transformed into a goddess of war, tall in the saddle of her white horse, Leicester walking next to her, carrying her helmet. Men streamed out of their tents, falling to their knees, awestruck at the splendor of their queen, who thrust her staff high into the air, eliciting a cheer from her army.

"My soldiers!" she cried, holding her silver staff high in the air. "I'm told we're to expect company soon. They've not been invited. They come to save our souls. But I say England has no need of Spanish prayers. So let them come with all the fires of hell—my soul is not for burning yet!"

By now, the entire army had gathered and at once rose up and cheered, the men's faces brighter than they'd been in weeks, a new energy and inspiration surging through them.

"I know I have the body of a woman, but I have the heart and stomach of a king—and a king of England too. So let them come. They shall find us ready. We have all England at our backs. We stand on English soil; we breathe the air of home. On such a field, will we not fight like giants? Will we not whip these ship-borne rats till they squeal for their lives? Will we not drive them back to the cliff tops, the great white cliffs of England, and make them jump?"

The ground shook as the men shouted approval and stomped their feet.

"I am come to stand with you today. To fight with you. And, if it's God's will, to die with you. Let them come! You and I have work to do today that will make England proud. And that work is victory!"

Her soldiers roared, holding their weapons—swords, pikes, axes, bows—up high above their heads. And as she looked at her army gathered at her feet, she found herself exhilarated in a way she'd never felt with any of her lovers. She was intoxicated and knew that no one would be able to take this sublime feeling away from her. This was something worthy of her fidelity, her heart, her love.

From the soldiers, a new chant had begun: *Gloriana! Gloriana!*

In the Channel, the wind had changed, sending sails flapping in a new direction as a storm churned the waters, buffeting the vast Armada and tossing the English ships in its waves. On board the *Ark Royal*, Raleigh and Drake, soaked by the spray whipped up in the wind, hurried along the deck. Their scheme was nothing that hadn't been done before, but Raleigh loved it for its elegant simplicity. Nothing threatened wooden ships more than the risk of fire.

"They've dropped anchor because of the storm," Raleigh shouted above the noise of the wind. "Now's our chance."

Drake nodded. "Parma could arrive at any moment. Luck to you."

Raleigh climbed into a small skiff and helped the sailors on it row through the rough sea to the *Tyger*, where he stepped onto the deck and started giving orders. Within minutes, he had pulled anchor, and the *Tyger*, along with seven other ships, was moving away from the rest of the fleet, heading straight for the Armada. Waves crashed against the deck, and the salt stung his eyes as he shouted orders to his men, feeling the slightest tinge of sentimental regret at what he was about to do.

He looked up at the tall masts, full sails, and remembered climbing the rigging to get a better view the first time he saw the New World creep up on the horizon. He blew out a long breath and carefully ran a line of fuses along the prow of the ship, gripping the side as he went. The wind was rising, and even the sturdiest sailors were having trouble staying upright as the *Tyger* was tossed by larger and larger waves. The fuses set, Raleigh picked up a barrel and joined his men pouring pitch over the deck, which was soon covered in a thick, sticky layer.

All was ready. He ordered his men off the ship and stood, holding a flaming torch, calmly surveying his target, drinking in a last look at the ship that had brought him so much glory, so much adventure. It was a good way to go, in dramatic fashion instead of slowly rotting at a lonely dock. He could not resist giving a crooked grin, then tossed the torch behind him, ran to the side of the ship and scaled down a swinging rope ladder as the deck burst into flame.

He squinted into a spyglass. The light from the burning ships revealed the chaos engulfing the Armada as the fire ships approached the Spanish line. The wind carried the sound of anguished shouts and desperate orders as they fired cannons and muskets, but to little avail. He saw them pulling up their anchors. The tight crescent formation they'd held for so long began to crumble as the towering Spanish ships moved in every direction with no semblance of order.

Raleigh turned his glass on to the *Tyger*, counting minutes as he watched. Any time now. A roar echoed off the waves as the ship's cannons, ignited by the pre-laid fuses, exploded as she crashed into the side of an enemy vessel. The hulls collided with a great splintering of wood. Masts bent with a hideous creak and then slammed into the deck, sending sailors scrambling to jump overboard.

He dropped the spyglass into his pocket and ordered his men to row, and with arms quickly growing stiff, they pulled against the choppy water, doing their best to ignore the cries of drowning Spaniards. Not all the fire ships struck their targets, but that was a minor detail. They'd succeeded in destroying the Armada's formation and opened up the seas to the rest of the English fleet. Drake and Howard would waste no time in finishing the job.

The night was filled with sounds of battle as cannonballs flew, wood split, and men died. Blood streamed off the decks of crippled ships. The quick, maneuverable English fleet darted through the water, mercilessly continuing their attack as the Spaniards did all they could to escape.

Raleigh continued to row until a shot landed in the middle of the skiff, killing one man and splitting the small boat's hull. A second cannonball followed almost immediately, and they were all plunged into the water, struggling to stay alive. Raleigh surfaced quickly and started to swim in the direction of the fleet, but it was an enormous distance to close.

Cannonballs and wood flying from destroyed ships came perilously close to hitting him as he swam through red-tinged water that was full of debris: battered pieces of wood, a lonely statue of the Madonna, a charred Spanish flag, and the drowned bodies of countless men. Worse, though, were the wounded, crying out for help as they slowly drowned. As the battle intensified, the smoke from the guns grew thicker, and soon Raleigh had lost sight of the English ships. He had no idea where to go.

He tried to swim forward but could not judge whether he was heading in a straight line. Movement was preferable to staying still, but he had to be careful not to exhaust himself, and he searched the water for a piece of wood that could serve as a float. That found, he continued on until he recognized one of the bleeding men in the water.

It was Calley, barely conscious, with a gaping wound in his shoulder. Raleigh swam around him, reaching around his chest and clutching him close. He could not hold both his friend and the wood, so he abandoned the wood and kept swimming, swallowed by the powder smoke, tossed by the churning sea.

Hours seemed to have passed, and his entire body hurt, pain screaming in his joints. A cannonball hit the water less than a foot from him, bringing with it a reinvigorating jolt of energy that coursed through him. He pulled Calley, whose breathing was growing progressively shallower, closer to him and swam on.

And then he saw it.

Through the smoke, the side of a ship.

He summoned all his strength and moved toward it, ready to collapse when he felt the wood of its hull. He shouted to the crew, though he knew they could not hear him above the cannons and tried to figure the best strategy for climbing on board.

Until he noticed something.

It was Spanish.

Now despair filled him, and Calley felt like an impossible weight, but he would not release his friend. Wood splintered near him and the ship in front of him began to tilt. This gave him hope—an English ship was within gun range. He needed only to determine which side of the Spanish galleon had been hit—then he would know, generally speaking, the direction from which the cannonball had come.

He swam back toward the hull, until he was so close he could easily touch it, and he looked up, hoping to see damage. Nothing. He followed the line of the ship until he reached the stern, which he could identify by feeling for the rudder. He continued around. Calley had begun to cough and Raleigh struggled to hold him higher above the water.

As he reached the other side of the Spanish ship, the waves grew rougher, but he could not tell if it was due to the storm or the battle. Exhausted, he treaded water next to the hull, balancing against it, hoping for a small measure of relief before continuing on.

There would be no relief.

A great explosion shook the ship above him. A cannonball must have struck the powder room. He pushed off from the hull and headed away from the galleon. It soon became evident he was going in the right direction, for although he could not see more than a few feet ahead of him in the water because of the thick smoke, he could now tell that cannons were being fired both in front of and behind him. He and Calley were in the middle of the battle.

His muscles burned, his lungs ached, and he lost his grip on his friend. Calley sunk under the water, Raleigh following him at once, grabbing for him desperately and dragging him back up to the top. Again, he held him around the chest and started to swim. Around them, the air, thick with the acrid stench of battle, thundered with the roar of guns.

He would not be able to keep this up much longer.

He had nearly started to despair when the wind blew, clearing the smoke, and he saw her, lit by the fires burning all around: a skiff, full of English sailors, men he recognized from the *Ark Royal*. He called to them, but they did not hear, and with a strength that surprised him, he moved quickly, honing in on them, not wanting to lose his sense of direction. Smoke settled again, and they were gone, but he kept swimming.

And then something hit the back of his head. An oar. It was the skiff. Pain exploded through him, but it was nothing compared with the exhilaration, the joy pulsing in his veins. With his free hand, he grabbed the side of the boat, whose sailors were now scrambling to help him, and he threw back his head and laughed before he handed Calley up to the sailors and then dragged himself on board.

As dawn broke, Raleigh, now back on the *Ark Royal*, leaned against the railing of the quarterdeck. Calley had been tucked into a berth and tended to by Howard's own physician; he would make a full recovery. Raleigh's own injury was minimal—a small cut on his head where the oar had struck him. He was tired, but that was part of battle, and he hardly noticed the pain lingering in his muscles from his long swim.

The Armada had scattered, but one ship had not fled so quickly as the rest and had been left vulnerable and alone. Raleigh climbed the rigging and quickly identified the vessel. He slid down the ropes, calling for Drake.

"It's the *San Martin*," he shouted as Drake rushed toward him. "Medina Sidonia's flagship."

"We must attack at once," Drake said.

"Give him no chance to escape." English losses had been heavy, and blood collected in the grooves of the deck. Raleigh ran to the guns, joining a crew who had lost their loader. A boy—a powder monkey—tossed him a bag of gunpowder, and he shoved it down the barrel, ramming it tight, then added the shot. The gunner added more, finer powder to the hole at the top of the cannon and prepared to light it.

They waited, just long enough to catch a glimpse of the *San Martin* through the smoky air. The gunner touched his match to the hole and the men pulled hard on the breeching ropes as the gun recoiled back at them. As soon as it had stopped moving, the sponger dipped his instrument in a bucket of water, saturating its lambskin end, and then thrust it into the barrel, twisting back and forth to put out any fiery residue so the gun could be loaded again.

Raleigh was ready with another bag of gunpowder. They repeated the process over and over, hardly able to see through the thick smoke whether they were hitting their mark. Shot flew around them, but the *Ark Royal* was spared serious damage as it continued sailing straight at the *San Martin*.

The remainder of the Armada had turned, captains scrambling to come to their leader's assistance, but they were met with a relentless battery of deafening guns as the English fleet pounded them. And on board the *Ark Royal*, it became clear that the Spanish answering fire was coming more sporadically, and this spurred on more rounds of attack until the air hung heavy only with the smoke of English cannons.

The Invincible Armada was defeated, fleeing north because they could not pass through the English line. Raleigh searched out Drake and the two men embraced, heady with their victory.

"You were right all along," Raleigh said, clapping Drake on the back. "God is a Protestant."

High on a hill above Tilbury, Elizabeth watched, the wind lashing her clothes and hair as she breathed in fresh air of the storm. Seeing the fire ships tear through the Armada had filled her chest with a hope that grew and blossomed into pure exhilaration when Drake's message arrived the next day:

> *There was never anything pleased me better than seeing the enemy flying with a southerly wind to northwards. God grant you have a good eye to the Duke of Parma; for with the grace of God, if we live, I doubt it not but ere long so to handle the matter with the Duke of Sidonia as he shall wish himself back at St. Mary Port among his orange trees.*

This was her triumph, everything for which she had prayed.

Making it sweeter still was the fact that she was not alone. Robert had climbed the hill with her, keeping back, but she could feel his eyes on her. She turned away from the sea and, tasting salt on her lips, wiped her face with the back of her hand, then motioned for him to come to her. He stood at her side, not touching her. She let her sleeve brush against his and welcomed the feeling of warmth that sprang from her heart into all of her limbs.

"So what say you, Eyes? It's quite a victory."

"Did you think for a moment God would abandon his anointed queen?"

She studied his face. They were so much older now than when they'd been in love, and she could no longer recognize every line, every crease, so she tried to memorize them now. His hair had thinned, turned gray, but he would always be handsome to her. "I had faith," she said. "But you know how I hate war."

"I do. I know you very well."

"You should never have done what you did in the Netherlands."

"Forgive me, Majesty."

"You would not be here if I hadn't already forgiven you." She looked back out over the sea. "It seems forgiveness is what everyone needs from me. Unless they're looking for money or position."

"I— I—" He stopped, gave her a tight smile. "I don't want to speak out of turn, but I know of the difficulties caused by your friend's marriage . . ."

"Do you refer to Raleigh's or to your union with that she-wolf?"

He drew a deep breath, looked at the ground. "I—"

"It's been nearly ten years, Robert. I'm quite over it."

"Yet you won't receive her."

"Why should I? She stole my love away from me." There was a cynical smile behind her eyes. "And being queen comes with the benefit of not having to forgive such transgressions."

"You've always had my love, always will. You were angry because I married someone I chose on my own instead of a woman you'd picked for me. What if I'd married the Queen of Scots, all those years ago, as you suggested?"

She reached up and touched his cheek. "I wish I had been the one next to you watching these wrinkles creep onto your face."

"You could have been," he said, putting his hand on top of hers. "Do you not think my heart was broken, too? I have loved other women, but none will ever hold the place in my soul that you do."

She felt tears coming but did nothing to stop them. Robert had seen her cry, knew her as well as—probably better than—anyone. "I have only done what I thought best for England, best for my people."

"And you are an extraordinary queen because of it. I simply wish it could have included what was best for you as well. You deserve happiness."

Now she turned away, covered her face with her hands. "The happiness of my realm is my own."

"I wished for you someone to share that joy. I wanted to

be that person. And when you wouldn't let me, I knew not what to do but look elsewhere. I am a weak man, Majesty."

"Elizabeth, Eyes. Today I will be your Elizabeth."

"And tomorrow?"

"Tomorrow I return to London. Alone."

"I can live on today for a long time," he said. "Come, let's celebrate your victory. Your soldiers are waiting for you."

Rumors had seized Europe before the battle in the English Channel was over. Bells rang throughout the continent, declaring victory for Catholic Spain. It was said that Parma had taken London, that Drake was a prisoner. Bonfires were built, and the people rejoiced at the downfall of the heretical English queen. She was burned in effigy, cursed as a demon, all with hearty measures of glee. It was only a matter of time before Philip would rule England.

But there were other voices, quiet ones, that told different stories. Stories of death and defeat, of scurvy and crippled ships. They were ignored, and Philip, lifted by the glory of God's success, ordered thanksgiving masses to be said. The chants of war that had echoed through the palace were replaced with joyous hymns.

Philip was in his cell, kneeling on the hard floor, offering prayers of thanks. He was startled when he heard voices outside the door, then a knock.

"Sire . . ." Four of his ministers, their heads bowed, stood in the corridor.

Philip rose to his feet. "What news?" he asked. One look at their drawn faces told him they brought nothing good.

"Medina Sidonia was forced to flee. The Armada scattered. We are defeated."

"Scattered?" His body went numb. "But they will fight again?"

"They regrouped, sire, after fleeing north, but are greatly crippled."

A second minister spoke. "More than a thousand of our men are dead, and the fleet has been savaged. We'll be lucky if seventy ships return to port."

"No more now," Philip said. "It is enough. I will come to you later." He brushed past them, rushing through hallways. There was no more sound of joyous hymns, and he could see that even his servants, who looked down as they pressed themselves against the walls to keep out of his way, had heard the news.

He would not despair. This was all God's will—a will that weak-minded humans could not always understand. He could not begin to comprehend it, but prayer, prayer would bring enlightenment, teach him why—how—he had failed God. Failed Spain. Failed the people of England, whose souls would suffer for eternity.

His soul was in need of great cleansing.

He'd walked to the nursery, but Isabella was not there. She was outside with her nurse, in the garden, and he found her there playing with her dolls. He bristled at the sight of the red-haired one that seemed to be her favorite. Anger filled him and he reached for the toy—a perfect image of the heretic Elizabeth—stopping his hand as he realized that he meant to crush the porcelain head. He murmured a quiet prayer, asking for strength and grace.

"What is it, Father?" Isabella asked.

"Walk with me, child," he said and took his daughter by the hand, leading her toward the basilica at the center of the palace.

The infanta did not protest but took her red-headed doll with her. "Are you making me Queen of England now, Father?"

"No, my dear. You will not be Queen of England."

"But I thought—"

"God wants you elsewhere, child. That is all. You will find understanding in prayer." They'd reached the church and marched through the nave, where Philip stepped in front of his daughter and knelt at the altar. He dropped down farther, abasing himself on the hard stone floor.

Behind him, the infanta stood, impassive, staring at her doll. She pulled its hair, covered its face with her hand, and then threw it to the ground. Philip heard the porcelain crack against the floor. He rested his forehead on the cool marble and started to sob.

Chapter 22

Bess was lonely and sick with worry for her husband. Rumors flew constantly about the battle—some said it was over—but she heard only what her servants knew. No one else was talking to her. Weeks had gone by with no word from Raleigh, and though she knew not to expect a letter—not from a battleground—she could not shake the terror of wondering if the next knock on her door would bring with it dreaded news.

Durham House, where she'd come after Raleigh's release from the Tower, was too large for a solitary woman, and the isolation was unbearable. She had been accustomed to days overstuffed with activity and had not realized how much she'd come to depend not just on the distractions of court but on the queen as a friend. Their relationship had always been lopsided—they weren't equals—but Bess had known she could trust Elizabeth, and it was this that had brought searing guilt to her every encounter with Raleigh. Betrayal had not come easy to her.

She'd not slept the previous night and now sat at a table, a blank piece of paper in front of her, pen in hand, trying to compose a letter to the queen. Crumpled on the floor were her previous efforts, all rejected. She wanted to apologize but also to make it clear that she was not begging for forgiveness she felt she did not deserve. She was glad Raleigh had chosen her, glad she was not the one heartbroken, but bitterly, bitterly saddened by the pain she had caused the queen.

She had made a selfish choice, but one that brought her an infinite happiness. An uncomfortable and familiar pressure built in her head as she scratched at the paper with her pen, not writing anything coherent, just drawing lines. Guilt was an unhappy companion. She dropped her forehead onto the table, wishing for a day without tears.

The door swung open. "Have you become a poet?" Margaret asked, coming to her side. "You're completely surrounded by papers."

Bess leapt from her chair and embraced her friend. "I can't tell you how good it is to see you," she said.

"I'm sorry I've kept away."

"I understand," Bess said, again feeling selfish. She didn't want Margaret to fall from the queen's favor, particularly if she were responsible for it. She could not bear to take on more guilt. "But you're well?"

"Yes, everything's fine," Margaret said. "I've missed you, though."

"And I you. More than you can imagine. How is the queen?"

"She was a terror for weeks. I hadn't really believed her feelings for Raleigh ran much beyond a typical flirtation. You know how handsome we all found him, how amusing. But he'd awakened something in her that had been dormant since Leicester."

Bess sighed; tears filled her eyes.

"Don't cry, Bess. What could you have done? Decided not to love him?"

"No. I'd always love him, but I could have chosen not to have him."

"For what? So that all three of you could be miserable?"

"I would have been the only one miserable. They would have been happy."

Margaret took her hands. "You're supposed to secure your own happiness, Bess."

"Not at the expense of others. Not when it hurts someone dear to you."

"Was it wrong of you to want him? To love him?"

"I knew she loved him," Bess said. "And yet I—"

"You can't control everything, Bess. Don't regret your decisions now."

"I don't regret it, Margaret. I just wish my joy didn't come with someone else's pain."

"I'm not here to make you melancholy. Messengers have arrived at court with news—the Armada has been defeated. The battle is over."

"My husband?" Her heart was pounding. She was almost afraid to ask the question. "Is he—"

"He's alive, Bess. He'll come home to you."

MARGARET'S NEWS MADE BESS soar. She could wait forever, knowing that he was safe, that he was coming back. For a day, she forgot even her guilt. Then the pains started.

She'd been walking by the river when she doubled over, crying out, a servant rushing to her side. She couldn't see, she couldn't think, couldn't move. Someone carried her to her bedroom.

She'd missed her husband before, but she wanted him even more now. Wanted him next to her, or at least waiting on the other side of the door, and she called for him whenever she could gather enough breath between the screams that came with each spasm of pain. Outside, cheers of victory bounced through the city, coming from Whitehall Palace, where the courtiers were waiting for their queen to return from Tilbury. The sound of their joy goaded her, their happiness taunting her as she suffered, hardly able to bear this agonizing feeling of being torn inside out.

It would not be so bad if he were with her. If it were his green eyes meeting hers instead of the cold gray ones of the midwife, who kept telling her to push. She couldn't push.

She was exhausted, spent, her muscles unwilling to listen to commands that her brain was hardly able to send. She couldn't even lift her hand to wipe the sweat from her brow, and here this woman expected her to push.

But just when she thought she could not stand to listen to the midwife for another second, it came with the force of an avalanche: an urge to push so overwhelming that she gripped the sides of the bed and cried out as if she would die. And then a pause, and more pain—a searing heat—and she pushed again, over and over in a furious rhythm until her shift was soaked with sweat and she thought her eyes would roll back in her head. She could no longer focus, only push.

And then it stopped, her body fell limp, and she panted, collapsed. And the wavering cry of a newborn child filled the room as all outside noise seemed to fade to nothing. She tried to raise her head but could not.

"A boy, madam," the midwife said. "Look at your son."

Now she did raise her head to look at the tiny body, the red face, and her face lit with a radiant smile.

A son.

ELIZABETH SET OFF FROM the palace almost before she'd finished reading Ursula's message. She'd cursed her rowers for being slow and lazy on the way and had snapped at her ladies with such ferocity that two of them had started to cry. Would that she could have flung them into the Thames.

When at last they reached Walsingham's house, she hardly recognized her Moor, but she knew at once that the foul odor that greeted her in his bedroom was the stench of death, and she choked back tears before anyone could see.

"Francis," Elizabeth said. "My old friend."

He spoke with difficulty, his voice raspy, weak. "I have served Your Majesty in all things."

"I know it, old friend. Don't leave me now."

"Always giving orders," he said.

"I couldn't have done anything without you. You've been more than a protector and advisor. I can't bear the thought of losing you."

He opened his eyes, did his best to smile. "You don't need me anymore. Permission to go—"

She shook her head, looking tenderly at him. "You always did do as you pleased, whether I wanted it or not. I've no doubt you'll do as you please now." Her heart felt as if it would split in two, and she knew she would not be able to hold her composure for long.

He closed his eyes once more as she stooped down to kiss his cheek, and his breath sounded like a rough rattle. The end was upon him; he would not be able to hang on much longer. Elizabeth squeezed his hand, glad for a last feeling of warmth in him, and rose to leave, knowing that his wife and daughter, who'd already begun to sob, wanted to grieve in private as much as she did.

William Walsingham's small, anonymous house was not easy to find. He felt safe hidden on the shabby street, but safety brought with it guilt. Guilt that he had been spared while his comrades had been executed. He'd fled to France, helped along the way by Catholic sympathizers. But although he should have rejoiced to still be alive, guilt was tinged with anger that martyrdom had been snatched from him. And now he had sorrow as a companion to his guilt. His brother had died in England.

William poked the fire burning in his grate and picked up a book, a half-eaten bowl of stew made from meat that was rather too close to rancid on the table next to him. A firm rapping on the door jolted him out of his reading, and half-distracted, still holding the book, he opened the door to find a stranger. A stranger whose voice was undeniably English.

"My brother? How is that possible?" It must be about his will. Surely he'd not been left anything, but perhaps his brother had decided to forgive him more completely, to let him have another chance with his family. William's eyebrows shot up; his mouth twitched. "What is it?"

"He asks your forgiveness."

"*My* forgiveness?" William stared, then understood, fear bringing sudden tears to his eyes. He gasped as the man plunged a knife into his heart.

Chapter 23

It had seemed to Raleigh that he would never get home. He'd gone with the ships that had chased the Armada north, making sure they would not turn back and try to attack England again. But now, at last, he was back in London, rowing on the Thames, Durham House in sight. He could hardly keep himself from standing up in the boat and shouting for Bess to come meet him.

She wasn't at the dock. His servants greeted him, but he hardly noticed, not pausing even to acknowledge them as he ran inside, calling for his wife.

"Upstairs, sir," a maid called to him. "In the bedchamber. She's delivered a son." A son. Every fiber of his body rejoiced as he raced upstairs.

She was in the bed, head propped up by a tall stack of pillows, the curtains pulled so she could see out the window. Dark circles ringed her eyes, but he'd never seen them so blue, so clear, and the smile, full of pure delight, that met him as he stood next to her was the most beautiful he had ever seen. It tugged at his soul. He sat on the edge of the bed and leaned over to embrace her, burying his face in her long hair as he slid his hand under the collar of her shift so he could feel the warm, smooth skin of her back.

He pulled back so he could look at her. "You've never been more stunning," he said.

"You're a disheveled mess," she said. "Is this what men look like after spending too long at sea?"

"This and worse." She put her hand on the back of his neck and brought him closer, kissing him, and the touch of her soft lips consumed him with pleasure sweeter than any he'd known before. When she stopped, he smoothed her hair, touched her face. "May I see our son?"

"Of course." She slipped out of bed and put her hand in his, leading him to a small basket, and his breath caught as he looked down on the baby. He reached for him, but she stopped his hand.

"Don't wake him," she said, an enormous smile on her face. "You can pick him up after he's done sleeping."

Tentatively, feeling almost scared, he held out his hand and touched the boy's tiny fingers, gasping when he felt their smoothness, knowing that there could be no love more pure than that filling him now. He turned to Bess and kissed her, then carried her back to the bed.

When the baby woke, he took him from the basket and held him gingerly, dancing slowly, crooning a soft song as he carried the child downstairs, not wanting to wake Bess, who had fallen asleep. He kissed his son's head and was about to sit down, when a servant entered the room.

"Her Majesty the Queen!"

Elizabeth entered the room slowly, wanting to appear formal and regal, letting no warmth creep onto her face. She'd debated coming at all but, in the end, felt that she must. Angry though she still was, she wanted to see him, wanted to see the child. She controlled her breath, keeping it even. Then, with a wave of her hand, she sent away servants and guards.

And there he was. Holding the infant. She had not expected this. It simultaneously cut and warmed her. "When was the birth?" she asked, crossing to him. He looked tired, thinner—battle-worn—but still handsome.

"Four nights ago."

"The mother is well?"

"Yes, thank God," he said.

"And the child?"

"My son is well." The pride in his voice made her smart.

"Your son . . ." She stepped forward, looked at the baby. "So the other Elizabeth has a child. You must be proud."

"Yes."

"I owe you thanks for your role in the battle. Drake tells me you were spectacular. A hero."

"I only did my duty," he said.

"And you saved the life of a friend."

"Is there anything you don't know?"

She could not help smiling at the easy tone of his voice, but she knew they would never flirt again. Moving away, she turned her back, not wanting him to see the pain etched on her face. "I thought once that you were the only man in the world who truly knew me."

"I loved you," he said.

"And did you love her too?"

"Yes."

"Is one woman's love not enough for you?" she asked.

"Is one man's love enough for you?"

She stood, silent, for a long moment. "No. One man's love is not enough."

"You have the love of all the people of England."

"That I do," she said. "And you? Do you still dream of your shining city in the New World?"

"Always," he said.

"I will not keep you from it. You'll have your warrant, whatever you need."

"Thank you, Majesty." His voice was full of love, and their eyes met. She let herself feel lost in them for the briefest moment, then squeezed his hand and turned to go. As she reached the door, she stopped.

"I'd like to give your son my blessing," she said.

"I would be honored."

She took the baby in her arms, holding him carefully, bending over him, her eyes brimming with emotion as she bit her lips to keep them from trembling. At last, she pressed her cheek to the tiny head, breathed in his buttery smell, and closed her eyes.

ELIZABETH WAS GLAD TO let plans for the celebrations of her victory consume her. Summer had ended, and the fleet and army were coming home as the mighty Armada, hopelessly crippled, made its pathetic way back to Spain. She'd consulted with Dr. Dee and settled on a date in November to progress to St. Paul's after a series of public holidays. She would present a new image of herself—Gloriana, the invincible queen.

"Majesty . . ." Sir Christopher Hatton stepped into the room, approaching her more cautiously than was his habit.

"What is it, Lids? You don't look yourself," she said.

"I—" He stopped and something about the look in his eyes—a look she couldn't quite decipher—scared her. "I bring news from Oxfordshire."

"Oxfordshire?" Robert's home was there, in Cornbury.

"It's Leicester, Majesty. He's dead."

The entire world went black for a moment. She felt herself stagger, could not draw breath. A pain like none she'd known before squeezed her heart and forced its way through her veins. "How?"

"He'd been ill."

"I know, but I never thought—" He'd written to her, saying he'd felt unwell and asking permission to go to Buxton, hoping that the waters there would cure him. She'd written back at once, telling him to go. The following day, she'd sent him one of her rings.

"I'm very sorry," Hatton said. He stepped forward, arms out, offering an embrace, but she pushed him back. She couldn't bear sympathy.

"No. No." She shook her head. "Please leave me. I must be alone." He obeyed at once, and when he was gone, she flew to her desk, upon which sat a letter she'd received from Robert only a handful of days ago.

> *I most humbly beseech Your Majesty to pardon your poor old servant to be thus bold in sending to know how my gracious lady does, and what ease of her late pain she finds, being the chiefest thing in the world that I do pray for, for her to have good health and long life. For my own poor case I continue still your medicine and find it amends much better than any other thing that hath been given me. Thus hoping to find perfect cure at bath, with the continuance of my usual prayer for Your Majesty's most happy preservation, I humbly kiss your foot. From your old lodging at Rycote this Thursday morning, ready to take my journey,*
>
> *by Your Majesty's most faithful and obedient servant,*
> *R. Leicester*
> *Even as I had written thus much, I received Your Majesty's token.*

She bit down hard on her fist as she read his words, then picked up a pen and wrote across the paper, "His last letter." The thought that there would be no more, that he was no longer there, far away but thinking of her, stabbed her. It was unbearable. Her Sweet Robin, her Eyes, gone. She fell to her knees and sobbed.

SHE SPENT DAYS LOCKED in her bedroom, refusing to see or speak to anyone. There was continual commotion outside her door, as courtiers and her councilors pleaded, trying to get her attention, begging her to take food, to open the door, to let someone comfort her. They did nothing but anger her, and she wished she could will the sound away, be left in peace to mourn. But a queen, as she was too frequently reminded, had no semblance of a private life.

She hardly slept, not that at present waking was much different from slumber. She was numb, couldn't think, did nothing but cry, silently now, and look out the window. On the fourth morning, as the sun rose, she felt ready to face them all. She drew herself up, read his letter again, then carefully placed it in a box next to her bed, where it would always be within easy reach. As she closed the wooden lid, the smooth surface cool to the touch, she stopped crying. She dried her face with her hands and then called for her ladies.

Her country needed her.

Her people needed her.

Their love would carry her, complete her, be with her forever.

Two months later, Elizabeth—Gloriana—was on her way to officially give thanks to God for bringing her victory over Spain. Bonfires had been burning for nights as all of England celebrated. And now, at the culmination of the festivities, every nobleman in the country jostled for a good position in the procession from Somerset House to St. Paul's Cathedral in the City. Bright banners streamed overhead as trumpets announced a spectacle that rivaled that of the queen's coronation nearly thirty years ago.

The Privy Council came behind the nobility, followed by state officers and soldiers. Every living person important to Elizabeth was there, including Raleigh and her old ministers—Lord Burghley, Hatton, Howard, and Drake. But she felt keenly the holes left by Walsingham and her dear Robert. She did not, however, succumb to sadness. She missed them, noted the feeling, said a quick prayer, and climbed into the open chariot that would carry her to the church. Its throne was surprisingly comfortable and she waved from beneath the canopy held in place by four pillars to the crowds gathered along the way.

As she approached Temple Bar, she slowed to allow the Lord Mayor and his aldermen to escort her through Fleet Street to the cathedral. The aldermen's scarlet robes moved in a blur past railings covered in blue cloth that separated her from the city's soldiers, saluting her as she went by. She felt the adoration in the cheers that greeted her, and a pleasing sensation of power swept through her.

They went up Ludgate Hill, and when they'd reached the church, the West Door was opened. She stepped off the chariot and approached the Bishop of London.

"Our glorious day has arrived," she said and then dropped to her knees in prayer. The crowd fell silent, but she felt no pressure to hurry. They could wait. Everything could wait. Only when she felt she'd adequately thanked God did she rise and make her way inside.

The sounds of a perfect hymn filled her ears as she walked down the lengthy aisle, above which hung banners captured from the Armada's ships. She felt a glow in her chest at the sight of them, these visible signs of triumph. She walked slowly, taking care to meet the eyes of as many of her subjects as possible, as always, wanting them to feel a personal connection to her—to think that she'd singled them out. It was as much for her benefit as theirs, though. She was soon intoxicated by the admiration on their faces.

After she had crossed the transept, she took her seat—hard wood in the north wall of the gallery's choir—and listened to the Bishop of Salisbury's sermon. Or pretended to listen. The truth was, she hardly heard the words, but their firm, joyous tone flowed through her, and she could not think of a time in her life when she'd been so content.

Soon the bishop had finished, and she rose and went to

the pulpit. She was dressed in gold, looking more like a goddess than a mortal, and a collective gasp greeted her when she stood, serene and regal, radiating power as she stood before her subjects. "I am called the Virgin Queen. And yet I have many children. You are all my children. There is no jewel, be it never so rich a prize, which I put before this jewel: I mean your love." Her voice soared as a heady mixture of love and power filled her. "I want no more wars. England is enough for me. I want no lordship over your souls. Only a free people can love. And in your love is my life."

She could feel that if they were not in a church, in the midst of a great ceremony, her subjects would have cheered. But they sat quietly, gazing at her, adoration traveling from their admiring eyes to her hungry heart. Their love would be with her forever. She would never need anything more.

Author's Note

This book is very fictional. Although I hope it accurately portrays the characters of Elizabeth and the people who surrounded her, it should not be mistaken for a history of the period. For example, Sir Walter Raleigh was not, in fact, at the battle with the Spanish Armada, and while he and Bess did elope, it was not until after England had defeated Spain.

The following books are excellent non-fiction resources:

- *Elizabeth the Queen,* Alison Weir
- *The Men Who Would Be King: Suitors to Queen Elizabeth I,* Josephine Ross
- *Elizabeth I,* Alison Plowden
- *The First Elizabeth,* Carolly Erickson
- *Elizabeth I,* Christopher Haigh
- *Queen Elizabeth I,* Susan Doran